AUGUSTUS AD 78
25 August

The ground shook today. Father says I mustn't fret – the ground often trembles in Pompeii. He *always* says that. But when we got home I saw that the crack in the atrium wall had got bigger. I slipped in the tip of my finger and wiggled it around to show him. "Yesterday, it did not go in at all," I said.

"It is just a crack, Claudia," Father told me. "The house is not going to fall down!" I do not know how Father is so sure. I am not! So I decided that I would begin a diary. In a diary you can write down everything you think and feel. And it will be my secret.

And now, oh Isis, goddess of a thousand names, guide my hand. May my words always be the truth.

We were in the Forum when it happened. We'd gone to the Forum so that Father could order grain for the bakery. Truly, I should have been home helping Mother, but she sent me out after I'd spoilt my work again. "Be off with you, Claudia," she said. "One day I hope the gods will teach you how to spin, for I cannot. But it seems it is not their will that you learn today."

And my, wasn't it busy! Everyone seemed to be in the

1

Forum this morning. Traders peddling everything from Egyptian granite to robes from Babylon, toga-draped officials, snake charmers and beggars. The air hot and heavy with the smell of sweat and spices. And over and above all the clamour, the shouts, the cries, the steady bang-bang of the builders.

"Take my hand, Claudia," Father said. "And whatever you do keep tight hold of Pollux's chain, or I fear we will lose him in such a crowd." (Pollux is our dog. He is supposed to guard the bakery, though Mother says the painting in our neighbours' house would be of more use.) Anyway, I tried to do as Father bid, though Pollux pulled me this way and that. He is always excited on market day. So many smells to sniff, titbits to tempt and dogs to fight.

All went well until we saw Ancient. Ancient usually begs at the Vesuvius Gate, for that's where the carts enter the city and the best pickings are to be had. Anyway, Ancient stretched out his hand and Pollux leaped forward – and I ran smack up against a man loaded down like a mule. "Ow!" I cried, putting up my hands to shield my head. Something – a pot – had knocked it and the contents all strewn on the ground. Didn't the trader just shout at me, while he scrabbled around, piling olives back into it. All dusty and dirty too now. Ugh! And then I realized that I'd let go of Pollux's chain. I looked round, but Pollux had gone – scampered away into the crowds. Father was *not* pleased. "That dog's more trouble than he's worth," he muttered as we searched for him, high and low.

2

I was near to tears when at last we found him – sniffing around the slave market. My, what a terrible place that is. Only human livestock is for sale there. We pushed through the crowds, past dawdling buyers and drooping slaves – the air as hot as Vulcan's forge by then – and there I saw Pollux, his nose resting in a boy's hand. The boy was in chains, his reddish hair matted, breeches filthy, but he was smiling, though I could not think what he had to smile about. One dirty hand rested on Pollux's head.

And what did I do? Pull Pollux away, snuff that smile out.

The slave master had been watching. I saw how greedily his eyes flickered over Father. A rich man. Aye. I will get a good price from *him*. He edged his way close, bowing at Father and me. "A fine boy, honoured master. He is next to be sold. If you can but just wait… A Briton. A barbarian – yes. But see – he is good with animals. A fine horseman too. And strong." He punched the boy's arm, and I winced.

Father put up his hand. "I am not buying," he said. "I am a baker. I have no need of a horse boy."

"He is strong, honoured master," the slaver wheedled, edging closer still. "He will turn the millstone faster than any donkey." He drew back his arm to punch the boy again.

"Come, Claudia," said Father, eyeing the slaver distastefully. As did I! *We* do not use slaves to turn our millstones! Behind us I heard the slave master shout harshly at the lad, kicking him up the steps to the rostrum where slaves are paraded

3

before they are sold. Father sighed. "Poor lad," he murmured. "Poor lad." And then, just as I was thinking how awful I'd feel if it was me, I heard Father exclaim: "By the gods, it's Vastus." I looked back. A small crowd of buyers had collected below the rostrum. And there, puffing up the steps, was a man in a spotless tunic, rings sunk deep into fat fingers. Vastus. Father's friend and one of the richest bakers in Pompeii.

Father wanted to stay then, so I crouched down, pretending to play with Pollux. I did not want to watch. I hate slave auctions – I hate to see people prodded and poked as if they are things – not people at all. Father was a slave himself once, and if he'd not been freed by his old master, I'd be a slave now too. I never forget that.

When I glanced up again I saw that most of the bidders had wandered away. Only two remained. One, Vastus. The other?

"The lanista. It is he who buys the gladiators for the arena," Father told me, pointing out a man in a rough brown tunic. "Vastus will not want to be outbid by a man like that. He will pay the price. The slave master will be pleased." I asked Father how he knew who he was. Father laughed. "He bears the scars of his trade," he said. He pointed out the scars on the lanista's face. "He will have been a gladiator himself once." I stared hard at the lanista, and it was as if he felt my gaze on him for suddenly he turned and stared straight at me. I shivered. Great dark eyes he had – the eyes of a man who had seen and done terrible things. Even now, writing hours later, I can still see those eyes.

I felt sure that he'd buy the boy but Father was right. It was Vastus whose head was bent close to the slave master. Vastus who was ordering the boy to be sent up to his house. I jumped up and clapped as the lanista stalked angrily away. To be sold as a gladiator is one of the worst fates that can befall a slave.

"That's a fine-looking boy you've bought," Father said, as we greeted Vastus.

Vastus clapped Father on the shoulder. "Aye, I'll get a lot of work out of him," he growled. I gave his back a hard stare. I am sure he will. Vastus does not treat his slaves well even though he was a slave himself once. I've seen the weals on their backs and legs. He told us that the lad's sister was also for sale. "The slave master tried to throw her in too," he said contemptuously. "He wants to be rid of her. And who would want a scrawny little package like that." He jerked his thumb at a girl crouching nearby. I am sure she heard – there was such hate and fury in the look she turned on him. It quite turned my stomach. And then I thought how I'd feel if it was me being parted from my brothers.

And that was when it began. Pollux was growling – as if he was angry too. Then suddenly he leaped forward, pulling me with him. Vastus stepped back hastily. Too hastily. He wobbled, and for one awful moment I thought he'd fall over. A man guffawed and Vastus went purple. You do not laugh at a man like Vastus. He scowled at me – as if it was all my fault! Father looked stern. "Pull that dog away," he commanded me.

I tried to do as he bid, but Pollux was straining forward so hard now that I could barely hold him. Link by link I felt the chain slip through my fingers. Suddenly Pollux stopped still, ears cocked. I heard something rumble – as if a wagon was driving straight across the Forum towards us. But there was no wagon and anyway wagons aren't allowed in the Forum. I'd barely time to wonder how odd it was when Pollux whimpered and the chain in my hands slackened as he crept back to cower round my ankles. I bent down to comfort him. As I stroked him I felt his body begin to shake – and then I realized that I was too.

"Father!" I cried, grabbing his arm as I felt myself topple. "The ground – it's shaking!"

On a stall nearby a pot wobbled and smashed to the ground. "By Jupiter," I heard the stallholder cry. "The girl's right. The ground *is* shaking."

"The gods are angry," people muttered, looking down at their trembling feet. But I found my eyes drawn north towards Vesuvius, the great mountain that looms over our city. That mountain has always scared me. At the top it is black and charred from the flames that used to devour it. When I was little I thought it was the home of the god Vulcan. I'd imagine him working at his forge, deep inside. And then suddenly I felt sure I was right. I told myself that I was being silly – Vulcan did not live inside Vesuvius. And what did the ground shaking have to do with the god of fire and smiths? But I had such a clear picture in my mind – it was almost as if I was sitting inside the mountain myself. I could feel the heat of the flames leaping from the forge fire; see the sparks fly as Vulcan smote his anvil, making the ground shudder all the way from Vesuvius to Pompeii.

And then the picture faded and I realized that the ground was still again. The stallholder picked up the shards of broken pottery. "Naught to worry about," he said, shrugging.

"Nay. You are wrong. Vulcan has sent us a warning," I heard an old voice quaver. Ancient! One wobbling finger pointed north – towards Vesuvius! People turned to stare. Ancient struggled to his feet. He spoke again, his voice stronger now. "The god is angry. We should heed his warning." He prodded his eyes. "Have you not eyes to see? Or ears to hear? Vesuvius is stirring."

"The old fool," I heard Vastus mutter next to us. "What has a little earth tremor to do with Vulcan, or Vesuvius? 'Vulcan is angry. Vesuvius is stirring!'" he mocked. "What nonsense! Anyway, why should Vulcan be angry? It is a mere two days since we did him honour."

That should have reassured me, but it didn't. There was something stirring in that mountain, there *was*. Something that boded ill for us. Ancient knew. Though what it was or how he knew I could not say.

I looked into Father's face. It looked serious, but he said nothing, merely drew me away from the crowd.

It is a wise man who heeds the words of the old, Father always says. They are nearest to the gods. I wish I could forget that.

7

My brothers had felt the tremor too, of course, but it did not frighten them. "We were at the bakery," Marcus told me. "Samius looked so funny – he nearly fell over." (Samius is our baker.) "Look, Claudia!" He clawed at the air, pretending to fall sideways. "And then his eyes went round and round – like this." He rolled his eyes. I hate it when Marcus does that! And then Sextus, my younger brother, went round the house jumping up and down to see if the ground would shake again until Father threatened him with the strap.

But later Sextus told me he'd squeezed his little finger into the crack too. "It's got bigger, Claudia," he said, his eyes all round and frightened. "Do you think our house will fall down? Marcus says it is sure to." Sextus is only seven, and I did not want to scare him, so I told him that I didn't think it would, though I am none too sure myself. Sextus put his arms tight round me. I held his chubby little body close, feeling how much I loved him. But my, I was cross with Marcus. He should not frighten his little brother, and I told him so.

26 August

An eagle flew over the town yesterday. And that is not a good omen! "Fausta saw it herself. She said it flew over the Forum," Mother told us.

Father tutted. "Well, we did not see it, did we, Claudia?" I shook my head, but unwillingly. That did not mean it wasn't true. Father sighed. "Yesterday was a day of many portents. As well as the ground shaking, I have heard of hailstones as big as a man's fist, the skies weeping blood. These marvels I have not seen. Still—" He hesitated, and I wondered if he was remembering what Ancient had said. "Fausta is old and we should heed her words. So we will make a special offering to our Lares this evening." But I swear I heard him grumble as he left to make the morning's call to his old master's son. "Women! What silly fancies they do have. Birds cannot fly when the air is still and the ground quakes." But I am sure that Fausta is right and she did see an eagle. Fausta has been our slave since I was a little girl. She does not make up stories, whatever Father thinks.

This evening, as usual, we gathered in front of the shrine to our Lares, the gods that protect our home. All of us were there – me, my parents and brothers and our household and bakery slaves. Even the cat wandered in from the bakery and sat in the shadows, his tail flicking back and forth.

The shrine to our Lares is set in a niche in the wall. It is quite grand, like a little temple. There are shutters on the outside, and when you open them you see little statues of our Lares inside. Behind the statues, on the wall, is a painting of them. Many of the other walls are painted, too. The paintings were already here when we moved to the house. In Father's study is a painting of Hercules, the hero who Father says founded Pompeii as well as nearby Herculaneum. The boys like that one best.

The family who once owned our house must have been very rich. They owned the entire house – not just part of it like us. Father says they ran away when the Great Earthquake hit Pompeii. The town was very badly damaged then – even now not all of it has been repaired.

Father looked very solemn, his head shrouded as we made the offerings. Sextus wrinkled up his nose as the sweet incense drifted over us. Sextus does not like that smell.

Fausta and the other slaves were huddled together. I do not know what Fausta was saying, but her lips moved constantly throughout.

28 August

I am so pleased! I have a whole scroll of papyrus to write on! I found it lying on the floor outside Father's study. I gave it back to him, but he says it is an old one and I may keep it. He unrolled it to show me. I could still see the faint marks of scrubbed-out letters. "Write only what others may read, Claudia," he said. I felt myself blush, thinking about the diary

I have begun. I pray Father never asks to read it. Anyway, what I write is private – between my diary and me.

I will write as small and neatly as I can so I do not use up the precious papyrus too fast. Then I will roll it up and hide it in the chest where I keep my most treasured things – the scarab that belonged to Mother's father and the baker's seal that Father gave me. It should be safe from prying eyes there. Anyway, I wear the key to the chest around my neck so no one can unlock it but me, and I have put a curse on anyone who dares to break it open.

29 August

It is almost too hot to write today. Chius swears you could bake the bread on the bakery counter. Mother even sent Xenia to fan me, but I have sent her away now. I wanted to write my diary. My diary is truly a joy to me – like having a secret friend. A friend who will never betray me, who I can say anything to.

We are to visit Uncle's farm tomorrow. It should be cooler in the countryside – so you'd think that would please me – but it does not. I am ashamed to write this, but I do not much care for my uncle. He is so strict and I find it hard to please him. Uncle works hard. He rarely sits down and even when he does, his hands are always busy, mending a basket or tinkering with a broken tool. He likes to keep us busy too. Tomorrow, Father says, we are to help pick the grapes. The last time I picked the grapes I got squashed grapes all over my tunic. You should have seen how Uncle looked at me. As if I'd done something awful. "What a clumsy child," he said, and then later I heard him mutter: "How will she ever hope to find a husband!" I do not want a husband – not yet awhile. So I hope that Father heeds Uncle's words.

I have another reason why I do not want to visit Uncle. His farm lies a few miles north of Pompeii, where the plain meets the mountains. It is a pleasant place, surrounded by sheds, storehouses and vines, but now I wish he lived almost anywhere else. I do not want to go anywhere near That Mountain.

30 August

I am home again – and I am glad glad glad! It has been a HORRIBLE day. First, we had to drive out almost on to That Mountain. (I sat with my back to it in the wagon so at least I did not have to look at it.) Then I had to spend much of the rest of the day inside Uncle's house, minding the slaves' babies, so that Asellina could help pick the grapes, and all because I got squashed grapes on my over-tunic again. Uncle is so mean.

I had to wash my tunic too. Uncle told Asellina to fill a tub with water, and then he set it down at my feet with such vigour that water slopped over the sides. "You must do it," he told me. "I cannot spare a slave today. And," he continued, as if a bright idea had just struck him, "you can mind Asellina's infants for her. Then she can do the work you cannot."

Uncle thrust lye into my hands to wash with. It is disgusting – a mixture of goat's fat and wood ash. Even now, my hands stink.

When I'd finished, I put my over-tunic out to dry on one of the scrubby bushes by the door. I could see the slaves as they tramped back and forth, big baskets of grapes in their arms. My brothers were shouting and laughing. I did feel sore.

By the time they trooped back to the house to eat, my tunic had dried, but the stains are still visible, pinky grey on white. Mother and I are to take it to the laundry tomorrow.

Uncle pushed a beaker of grape juice over the table towards me. "Straight from the vine," he said gruffly, his lips curving into something resembling a smile, as if he was sorry for his earlier surliness. Uncle's hands are as gnarled as the vines he tends, the nails chewed to the quick and rimmed with soil. Father's are soft and smooth – the hands of a younger man – yet Father is the older of the two brothers.

Then we tucked into bread and fresh goats' cheese.

I listened as they talked about the tremor. "Felt it here too," Uncle said. He hopes there will not be another great earthquake, like the one sixteen years ago. "Six hundred sheep died then," he said, shaking his head. "It was a bad thing for us farmers." A bad thing for all of us, I thought. If they felt it here too, nearly on Vesuvius. What was it Ancient had said? "Vesuvius is stirring." I felt myself shiver.

"Many upped and left after that," Uncle went on. "I was young then, but now…" He sighed.

"Farming is a young man's work," Father said carefully. "And you are not young." Father worries about his brother. He is ageing fast, and tired. I felt sure I knew where the conversation was leading. I looked at Mother, my eyes beseeching. Please, do not ask Uncle to live with us. Please! But, sure enough: "There is always room in our home for you," Mother said gently.

Every year now they ask Uncle this.

Uncle pushed away his plate. "I will live and die on this farm," he told us, thumping his beaker down on the table. He did not thank Mother and Father, but he smiled – and it was a proper smile. Not the half-hearted grimace he'd given me. Uncle's face softens when he smiles. But I am very glad he does not want to live with us.

My face must have shown what I thought because Mother said I should show Uncle more kindness. I'd be kinder to Uncle if he were kinder to me! "Your uncle may be gruff and grim, but he is lonely. Think on it. His wife and children are

14

all dead," she said softly as we drove home in the wagon. "Who will look after him when he grows old? We are all the family he has. Try to understand." And she sighed, and I felt certain that she was thinking about her own family – her brothers and sisters. Mother has seen none of them since she was a child.

31 August

This morning Mother took me round to Stephanus's laundry. Under my arm was tucked my still-stained over-tunic. Stephanus's is not the nearest laundry to us, but Mother says it is the best. "They will bleach it white again," she told me. "Stephanus is master of his craft."

I am thankful that laundering is not Father's craft. And that we do not live next door to a laundry! Outside there are always tubs of urine. Mother says it's used to bleach the cloth. When the tubs are full you can smell them halfway down the street. Ugh!

The entrance door opened and a girl came out. I watched as she picked up one of the tubs in hands that looked red and chapped. I felt sure I'd seen her somewhere before, but she did not even look at me. She had reddish hair caught back in a knot and her skin was fair, unlike Mother's and mine. Ours is as dark as a ripening olive.

"They won't just clean the tunic," Mother told me as we followed the girl inside. "They can tease out any fibres that get tangled in the process – and press the garment for us too." She pointed out the two big screws that work the iron press.

I sighed quietly. How often has Mother told me this? A hundred times? "It is important you know how things are done, Claudia, so that when you have slaves of your own they will respect you," she said. She's told me that before, too.

Steam billowed into the courtyard. As it cleared I could see small girls and boys trampling the clothes in tubs to rinse them. What a horrid job that must be. Afterwards the cleaned garments are usually dried on a terrace over the atrium but Stephanus's laundry is so busy that sometimes garments are laid out on the roadside.

Mother showed the laundress the tunic, explaining about the grape stains. "The little miss spilt her juice, eh," she cackled. "Well, we'll see what we can do." She whisked it away.

On the way home, we stopped at the bakery to collect our bread, and I filled Pollux's water bowl. He lapped up the water thirstily, and I looked at Samius accusingly. I am sure Samius does not look after Pollux as he should. Then I remembered the donkeys that turn the millstone, so I checked their water too. But their trough was almost full.

Mother's eye was on the row of figures scratched on the bakery wall. If a customer does not pay at the time of purchase, a mark is made by the counter. It is crossed off when the customer returns to pay. There were not many marks crossed out on this row. It was almost as long as the queue outside. "And no wonder, if they get their bread for free," I heard Mother murmur. But I think we bake the best bread in Pompeii. And that is why the queue is so long!

SEPTEMBRIS
1 September

It is hard finding a private place to write. Today I had such a scramble to put away the scroll before my brothers burst in to see me. I tucked it under my bolster. I do not want my brothers to know about my diary!

The boys had their wooden swords in their hands. I put my hands to my ears to shut out the clatter.

"Why didn't you tell us about the slave auction?" Marcus demanded, lunging at Sextus. "Gaius told us the lanista was there." I told him I'd forgotten about it. The tremor had put it quite out of my mind.

Marcus snorted. How like a girl, his eyes said.

"Gaius's father's bought a British slave. He's working in the new bakery," Sextus said, waving his sword about. I ducked.

17

"Gaius says the Britons are savages. Gaius says people are afraid of them. Gaius says he's not afraid. Gaius says…"

"Enough!" I cried. I made a grab for Sextus's sword, but he leaped backwards out of my reach.

"I bet he's a fine horseman," Marcus said. "They say all the Britons are."

"If he had been sold to the gladiator," Sextus said, "he could have fought from the chariot."

"Better to be sold as a charioteer." Marcus's eyes went all dreamy.

"Stupid!" I said. "Charioteers and gladiators get killed. Far better to be sold to a baker."

"They were going to buy the boy's sister too," Marcus began. "But…"

"He chopped off her hair and bought that instead!" Sextus shouted.

"No, he didn't," Marcus said. "Gaius was just bragging. He says they're so rich they can have anything they want."

They danced away. And now that I am on my own again I have been thinking about that girl and her brother. I'd hate it if someone cut off my hair. Slaves' hair is often sold to make wigs for rich Romans. And that red-brown British hair is much prized by ladies in Pompeii.

2 September

I have made a resolution today and I am writing it in BIG letters so that I will see it whenever I unroll the papyrus. That will make it all the harder for me to break. So:

I WILL STOP WORRYING ABOUT THE TREMOR AND I WILL STOP POKING MY FINGER INTO THAT CRACK.

Anyway, many days have passed now since the ground trembled, and the crack has grown no bigger.

But, oh my – what a lot of papyrus I have used writing in such big letters! Claudia, you are stupid!

4 September

I took a big meaty bone round to the bakery for Pollux today. Samius was at the counter, serving. "Wretched dog," he growled, wiping his hot face. "Never stops barking. Kept us awake half the night." I'd not heard him, but Mother says I'd not wake even if the house fell down.

Samius rents the upstairs flat, while the slaves sleep in the bakery. Father says he is a good worker, though my, he likes a grumble. He rubbed his eyes. "Ye gods! How that dog can bark! Woke up baby and half the neighbourhood too, I shouldn't wonder. Three times I thought we was being robbed, or about to be murdered where we lay. Three times I had to go downstairs, unlock the bakery and go outside. Took my big club with me. And what did I see? Nothing!" Samius gave Pollux a hard stare, but Pollux merely wagged his tail. Samius grunted and hollered for Chius out the back.

Chius came running to the counter, a basket of loaves in his arms. I tried not to look at his ears. They're so big I wager you could lay a loaf on each of them. Chius's eyelids were red as if he hadn't slept much either.

I love our bakery – I love everything about it, the bustle, the smell of hot bread, even the braying of the donkeys as they are yoked to the millstone. When I was a little girl we lived in the upstairs flat. Mother says it was a hard life then. No kitchen where we could cook hot food. In winter rain often drove in through the entrance. In summer the flat was both hot and dusty. But what I remember best is the smell of freshly baked bread wafting upstairs – it was the first thing I smelt when I woke. Mother remembers other smells too. Horrid it was, she says. And nowhere to wash things properly, or get rid of the rubbish.

When I turned seven, Father let me bake my own loaf of

bread. I was so proud of myself! I climbed up the steps to the platform and Father held tight to my legs while I tipped the grain over into the hole at the top of the mill. The flour mill is made of two hard stones, like upturned cones, one on top of the other. Some bakers use slaves to turn the millstones but ours are always turned by donkeys or mules. Father was once yoked to the millstone, when he was a boy. He rarely talks about that time, and says he will never treat another human like that. Sometimes we have to hit the donkeys to make them walk. "Ee-aw," they go. "Ee-aw," I shouted back that day, and Father laughed. The ground flour trickled out the bottom. Then it was sieved and mixed with water in a big stone basin. Father took hold of one end of the wooden paddle, and then he put one large hand over my little ones and helped me knead the mixture. Afterwards, it was put on one side to "rest" for a time. When it was ready, Father gave me a lump of dough and I wrapped the sticky stuff in a cloth. He showed me how to shape it into a round, and mark it into triangle-shaped portions. Then I stamped the loaf with his seal. "Not too hard, Claudia," he said, as I pressed down into the dough.

The oven was already hot. It gets lit long before daybreak, so the bread's baked and ready when customers come by for their morning loaves. Samius burns vine faggots in the oven to heat it. There are always plenty to be had, as vines grow abundantly near the city and on the mountains.

I placed my loaf on a wooden paddle and Father helped me slide it into the oven, shutting the oven door quickly to keep in the heat.

"When the sun god Apollo has driven his chariot to the top of the sky, we will take it out," he said. In our house now we have a sundial to tell the time by. But even without that Father and Samius always seem to know exactly when a loaf or cake is baked and ready.

I could not wait to see my loaf. I ran in and out of the bakery, pulling at Father's arm and asking if it was ready. Halfway through the baking time, the loaf was taken out, and I sprinkled water on top to brown it.

When the loaf was baked, Father took my hand in his and led me up to the oven. "Your first loaf," he said. "We must mark the day." He wrote something on the wall. I could not write or read then, and so I asked him what he had written.

"On 1 April I made bread," he said, and smiled at me.

I was very proud of that loaf! It had a shiny brown top. We had it for lunch that day, and I told Father that I would like to be a baker, like him, when I grew up. Father pinched my ear and told me that I had a lot to learn still. But now that I am thirteen and practically grown up I'd still rather be a baker like Father than a housewife like Mother. But then I'd rather be almost anything than that.

6 September

Oh joy – today I was released from the chores I hate. Isis, I thank you.

The morning began like most of my mornings do. As soon as we'd breakfasted, Mother told me to pull up a stool close by her. My insides were shrinking as I sat down next to her. I knew well what lay ahead of me. Spinning. The task I hate most.

It was still barely light so Mother lit the lamp on the tall stand next to me. The flame flickered unsteadily on its wick, but I could see the basket on the floor by my feet, brimming with hunks of sheep fleece. By the time the sun was high, all those hunks should be spun thread. I glowered at them. For the hundredth time I wondered why I had to spend my mornings spinning and weaving. You can buy clothes ready-made from the shops. We do not need to make them.

Mother handed me the wooden distaff. "It is important you learn how to spin and weave, Claudia," she said, as if she had read my mind. She attached a clump of fleece to the distaff for me. "When you marry..." she paused and I tried not to grimace. I hate it when Mother talks about me marrying "...when you marry you must know how things are done so that your slaves do not cheat you. I am grateful that I learned the skills I need to look after my family."

I held the distaff steady in my left hand, as Mother showed me. In my right I held the spindle. I pulled down a strand of wool, twisting it and winding it onto the spindle. But – oh Isis! – how tangled my fingers got. How knotted the thread.

This morning, too, the chattering outside distracted me. Each morning Father pays a call on his old master's son, and attends to any business he has for him. And by the time it is light enough to blow out the lamps, there are all sorts of people waiting to see him. People who need a favour, or who have fallen on hard times. It's a sort of help each other system. I will help you, if you help me.

It was light enough now to spin without my lamp. I blew it out, shifting my stool to catch the best of the light.

After I'd shifted my stool for the second time, there were few hunks of fleece left in the other baskets. Mine was still nearly full. I looked at it with hate. Why could I not learn to spin like Mother and the women? Why was my thread all knotted, while theirs was so fine and smooth?

Outside, meanwhile, the chattering had grown louder. Amongst the eager clamours and pleas I picked out Father's voice, calling for quiet.

He appeared in the doorway, and beckoned to Mother. I watched them, standing close together, absently twirling the spindle between my fingers. Then suddenly I felt it plucked from my hand.

"Come with me, Claudia," Mother was saying. "I have another task for you – one I think you will like better." What, I wondered, might that be? What domestic task did I do well? She led me past men still dawdling hopefully in the atrium – and into Father's study, a room I never dare enter without permission.

"Myrinus is sick, and your father needs copies made of these letters," Mother told me. "He tells me he has given you a scroll on which you practise your writing. So, let us see how well you have practised." I gasped. Me – to copy Father's letters! Me! Mother sat me on a stool and passed me the wooden board on which the letter was written. In front of me too was a roll of papyrus. It was a new scroll, unlike the one I write my diary on. I dipped my pen into the pot of ink at my side and began to write. My, I felt proud to be so trusted.

I could feel Mother's eye on my work as my pen scratched across the papyrus. When I had finished she read the letter aloud carefully, her finger moving slowly across the scroll. Sometimes Mother helps Father with the business accounts. She can count well in her head, but she was enslaved very young, so she did not learn to read and write as well as me.

"You write very neatly," she said, passing me another letter. "You have practised well."

At lunch Mother praised my work to Father.

Father helped himself to a fig.

"It seems we have a scribe in the family," he said, smiling

at me. "So, you practise your writing, child?" I mumbled that I did, blushing as I thought about my diary and the things I have written in it.

Father says I may write his letters until Myrinus is well again. I threw my arms round his neck. Thank you, Father. Thank you, Mother. May the gods honour you.

8 September

At last I have some time to myself. Ever since I got back from the baths, I have been bursting to write my diary.

We go to the baths most days. Father insists. "A healthy mind in a healthy body," he's fond of saying. Slaves carry our strigils, oils and sponge sticks. I skip ahead, dodging clumsy elbows. As we draw near I hear slaves bawl, gongs clang – the baths are now open. Mother lifts her tunic delicately, stepping from stone to stone across the street – wrinkling up her nose at the smell. And my, it stank today. It's often bad in the Street of Abundance. The street is lined with shops and there are flats above, so all sorts of stuff gets chucked into it – dirty water, food scraps – and worse! Sometimes slops tipped from the flats fall onto the food counters of the shops below. Ugh!

There are several public baths in Pompeii, none very far from home. Today we went to the Stabian Baths. They are the oldest, Father says – built long ago, before there was a Roman Empire. They were badly damaged in the Great Earthquake. Only the women's baths are open now.

Outside the baths, a workman on his knees was plastering cracks in the stonework, a basket of wet mortar beside him. Scaffolding had been erected and more men were working higher up on the wall. Was it old damage they were repairing or had the building cracked again when the ground shook? I screwed up my eyes, but the glare from the sun made it difficult to see anything properly.

All sorts of people gather at the baths – not just bathers. Here you can get almost anything you want. Your body rubbed, even your hair plucked! Olives, ripe figs – whatever you fancy, it's for sale. "Ripe cherries! Pompeii's finest," a streetseller bawled next to me. Flies swarmed eagerly over them. Pompeii's finest they were not!

Litters were bumping up to the entrance, borne on the shoulders of burly slaves. One came to a stop next to me, wobbling as carefully it was set down. A slave drew back the curtains and a sloe-eyed girl peeped out. Her eyes fell on me. "Claudia!" she exclaimed.

I stared back, speechless. "Aemilia," I got out at last. Aemilia is barely six months older than me. To think of it! A mere girl – to travel in such state.

Aemilia clicked her fingers and litter and slaves disappeared round the corner of the baths. "Father doesn't like me to travel around the city by foot," she told me. "He says it's Not Safe. Not now I'm a young lady." She giggled, and I rolled my eyes. Once we were the greatest friends but Aemilia is far too busy now pretending to be grown-up.

Another litter was set down next to us, and Aemilia's mother Pompeia stepped out. She gave us barely a nod before sweeping up to the entrance. Now they are so rich I am sure Pompeia thinks we are not grand enough for them. Behind her, two slaves trailed, laden with oils, perfumes, towels and boxes for Pompeia's jewellery.

The women's baths are towards the end of the courtyard, near the old waterwheel. We undressed in the changing room leaving the slaves to mind our clothes – there are as many thieves as bathers here – and wandered together into the warm room.

Mother was talking to Pompeia. I could not help staring at her hair. It was grey and wispy. Pompeia had taken off her wig but I could not remember what colour it was. Was it red? Had a wig been made for her of that slave girl's hair?

Aemilia was chattering away. "Father's bought a new slave," she said. "Just think, Claudia." She lowered her voice to a whisper as a slave came to oil us. "He's a barbarian – from Britain! Father says his sister was also for sale. He thought about buying her too, until he discovered that she was left-handed. And, he said, we don't need bad luck like that in our house."

A blast of hot air hit us as we entered the hot room. Steam swirled round us. Sweat poured off me. I slipped on clogs to protect my bare feet from the burning hot floor and groped my way over to the side of the room. I gulped some cold water. So that was the true reason why Vastus had not bought that girl. Why had he not said so? Left-handedness is unlucky. Who would buy a left-handed girl? Especially on that day. The day the ground trembled. A day of such strange portents... The beaker trembled in my hands. I put it down hastily. Aemilia was still chattering about the slave. Had nothing that happened that day bothered her? "So handsome," she was saying as we clambered into the hot bath, "or he would be, if he were less sullen."

Boys! That's all Aemilia thinks about now.

We returned to the warm room where slaves rubbed oil on us again and scraped us clean. Then back to the changing room, where Aemilia splashed cold water over herself. I plunged into the pool, but I clambered out again fast. My, it was icy! Then Aemilia left us to lie in the courtyard. She asked if I wished to join her, but her friend Iunia was there, and I cannot abide Iunia. She is even sillier than Aemilia. Anyway, I wanted to be alone to think, and it was far too hot to lie in the sun.

All the way home Aemilia's words hammered against my head.

We do not need bad luck like that in the house.

And then: *what did all those portents mean? What was going to happen to us?*

I could barely eat a morsel at lunch. Mother cast little worried looks at me, and each time I said no to one dish, she just passed me another. At last I told her that I was too hot to eat. I am sure she didn't believe me, for I have a prodigious appetite.

9 September

I have had the most terrible dream. It frightened me so much that I could not concentrate at all on my work. Mother was cross, so I pleaded that my head ached. She laid her cool fingers against my forehead. "It is hot, child," she said, looking thoughtful. I was afraid then that she would give me medicine. Mother's medicine usually makes me feel worse, so I told her I'd feel better if I lay down for a while.

As soon as she had gone, I pulled the key from around my neck and tiptoed quickly over to the big chest where I keep my clothes. I burrowed deep inside it until I could feel the hard surface of the chest where my diary is stored. Fingers trembling in my haste I unlocked it, pulling out the scroll of papyrus.

By writing everything down I hope to rid my mind of my dream – else my head will begin to ache in earnest.

This is my dream. I was in the Forum. All around me bits of masonry were toppling over. I tried to dodge the falling statues and pillars, but my feet felt stuck to the ground – the way they do in dreams. Overhead the great wings of an eagle flapped. The sky was growing as dark as night. In the distance sparks lit up the dark sky. Vulcan was striking his hammer so hard and angrily that flames were shooting right out of the top of Vesuvius.

I awoke then, hot all over. My old nurse Fausta was gently shaking my shoulder. "What ails you, child?" she asked me. "You were screaming fit to wake the gods."

"It washt the dream," I mumbled into her shoulder, eyes still tight shut. "Oh Fausta, it was the eagle, and…" I stopped talking and clung tightly to her, too afraid to open my eyes, afraid what I'd see if I did.

But why was I so frightened? Had I glimpsed what the future truly held for us?

Fausta put a finger to my lips, then waddled out of the room, muttering to herself. "Here," she said, returning. "Eat." She thrust a hunk of bread and beaker of milk into my hands. "If it is a bad dream you wish to speak of, first you must break your fast. Or bad luck will stalk you."

I took them, and did my best to swallow, though I nearly choked on the bread.

Fausta stroked the damp hair out of my eyes. Her wise old eyes probed mine. "Now you may begin," she said when I had finished.

I drew a deep breath, and told her everything.

Afterwards Fausta was silent so long that I felt even more frightened. But I had to know if what I feared was true. "Did you see an eagle?" I asked at last.

"Yes, child," she said quietly.

"What does it mean?" I whispered.

"Our fate lies in the hands of the gods. It is not for us to question." I looked hard into Fausta's eyes, trying to fathom her meaning. Fausta has the most curious eyes. One eye sees what everyone else does. The other is clouded, but I am sure it sees things that no one else can.

I sat on the edge of my bed, legs swinging, while Fausta helped me put my hair up into a bun on the nape of my neck. One by one I handed her the pins I'd been given for my birthday. They were pretty – bone, tipped with coloured glass. Fausta was chattering away as if she sensed I was still uneasy. "Pretty pins for a pretty girl. Here. Look," she said, handing me my bronze mirror. I stared into its polished surface. I do not think I am pretty. "Such soft hair you have, child," Fausta said gently. I mumbled something, and slipped down off the bed, but I felt far from comforted. Had Fausta seen what I had? A city destroyed for the second time?

Is our city doomed? Is it?

Oh Claudia, what a thing to write! I will see those words every time I unroll the papyrus. So I will put a line through them – there! It is done – and now I will do my best to forget that such a terrible thought ever entered my head.

10 September

Poor Marcus! Father beat him today. He had fought Sextus so he deserved to be punished, but I hated to hear the thwack thwack of Father's cane. When I next saw Marcus his tunic was stuck to his back, but he had borne the beating as a true Roman should.

I tried to comfort him. I brought out my knucklebones, my ball, even my marbles, but Marcus would not play. He drew his arm across his face. "Sextus provoked me – but no one believes that," he said. So I said that whatever Sextus had done, he should not fight a child smaller than himself, but that I was proud he'd borne his beating bravely. Then Marcus told me he had seen two mice in his room.

"We could race them," I suggested. Marcus brightened. "We could make two chariots and harness the mice to them."

But could we even find them? Not they. Marcus suggested we send in the bakery cat, but when I went round to fetch it, Samius told me it had vanished too.

I brought Pollux back with me. "What use will he be? He can't catch mice!" said Marcus scornfully.

I told him I was trying to teach Pollux tricks. Marcus

looked at me as if I was mad. "You could more easily charm a snake," he said.

I threw my ball.

"Show him, Pollux," I said protectively.

Pollux leaped up and caught it. "See," I said proudly. I put out my hand to take the ball back, but would Pollux drop it? No. In vain we wrestled him for it but Pollux darted away, the ball still held firmly in his teeth. Round and round the atrium he raced. Marcus laughed and laughed and soon he was rolling on his back on the floor. He sat up fast though. My, it must have hurt.

I took Pollux back to the bakery and we sat quietly, tossing knucklebones. Marcus told me that he did not want to be a baker when he grew up, and I confided that I did not want to be a Roman housewife.

"I wonder what the future truly holds for us," I said, toying with the knucklebones.

"Let's find out," Marcus said. He took the knucklebones from me. "Let's throw the knucklebones. If I throw a Venus, I won't be a baker." We looked at each other, giggling nervously as we shut our eyes.

The knucklebones clattered to the floor. Slowly we opened our eyes.

We stared at them, and then at each other – eyes wide. Marcus spoke first.

"A Venus," he whispered, awed.

I felt most peculiar. Why had we done such a thing? Why had we tried to find out what the future held? It is not wise to meddle with the fates. Marcus turned a cartwheel. "I won't be a baker!" he exulted. "Maybe I will be a charioteer."

"Don't be silly," I said uncomfortably. "Of course you'll be a baker."

He scowled, and held the knucklebones out to me. "Come on. It's your turn."

"No!" I said, and pushed his hand away. "No. I don't want to play any more."

Marcus shrugged and said that all girls were stupid, and he did not know why he was playing with one – especially his sister.

I stuck out my tongue.

"Fishwife," he muttered.

"Baker," I retorted.

"That's not what the knucklebones say," he answered haughtily, sweeping out of the room.

At dinner we still weren't speaking to each other.

"What is the matter with you, children?" Mother asked, after we'd pushed away honey cakes – our favourite. I looked at Marcus, and Marcus looked at me, and then Sextus looked at Marcus. We began to laugh, and Father and Mother looked at each other and laughed too. But inside I was still feeling peculiar. I wish we hadn't played that game.

I wish Marcus had not thrown a Venus. And Samius says the cat has not come back. Is that another bad omen for us?

11 September

Fausta roused me early this morning. I grumbled and pushed her away – head still thick with sleep. "Up with you, sleepy one," she said. "Or you will miss the dawn ceremony at the temple."

I leaped out of bed at once. Last night Mother had told me she'd take me to the Temple of Isis. I'd been so excited that I'd tossed and turned, falling asleep only to wake again as the carts began to trundle through the city. Not even I can sleep then.

The Temple of Isis stands to the south of our home. It was terribly damaged in the Great Earthquake, but unlike many other buildings in Pompeii was soon rebuilt, by a wealthy freedman. He must be very rich if he could afford to build such a beautiful temple. Father says he did it to get his son elected to the town council.

However early we arrive, there always seem to be people ahead of us. Today we were so far back in the crowd that even when I stood on tiptoe I could not see into the temple courtyard. But the temple itself is at the top of a flight of steps so when the darkness lifts even I can see in. There are statues of the Egyptian gods Isis and Osiris and paintings all around the temple walls. In the paintings are tiny people that Mother says are called pygmies, and crocodiles, and a bird with a curved beak, even a god with the head of a dog. Mother always says that the paintings remind her of home. When I was little I thought that Egypt must be a strange and frightening place.

In front of me the long white robes and shaven heads of the priests gleamed palely. *All* the priests' hair is shaved off – even their eyebrows. When the sun is fully risen and you can see their faces properly they do look odd.

All around us people were singing and shaking rattles in the goddess's honour. The high priest turned to break the seal and draw back the bolt on the door to Isis's sanctuary. As he lifted the image of the goddess to us, I felt the hair stand up on my arms. Mother's head was bent and I shut my eyes, only opening them again when I felt the darkness behind my eyelids lift. In front of me the temple glowed as the shadows peeled away. The fears I'd been harbouring seemed to be slipping away too. The sun had risen again. Another day granted to us.

"No matter how dark the night, the sun always rises," Mother said softly.

I slipped my hand into hers.

"Do you feel better now?" she asked me. I nodded. How is it that mothers just know if something ails you?

13 September

The most awful thing happened at the Temple of Jupiter today.

A bull bellowed as it was led to slaughter.

The trumpeters and flautists played loudly, as if they were trying to drown out the sound. But everyone must have heard it – everyone, that is, except the elderly priest conducting the ceremony. His assistant bent his head close and whispered to him. Around us people were growing angry. They began to hiss and I heard a clatter as something was thrown. And they were right to be angry. If the sacrificial rites are not properly observed – even if a bull bellows when it shouldn't – the gods may be displeased and refuse to protect us.

So the ceremony had to begin all over again. Back the bull was led, poor thing – eyes blinking placidly, mercifully unaware of its fate. I watched as the sacrificial knife was drawn down the bull's back. But as soon as I saw the priest raise his hammer, I shut my eyes tight. I cannot bear to watch its killing.

"Why do you shut your eyes?" a girl's voice piped next to me.

"Because I do not like to see animals suffer," I said, eyes still tight shut.

"It is done so that the gods protect us," the girl said. As if I didn't know!

I opened my eyes and gave her a look – and then shut them quickly again, but not before I'd seen the bull slump and blood spurt everywhere. Ugh!

15 September

Mother has bought me a new tunic – it is very long, like a proper grown-up stola. I have just tried it on – and I hate it. We went to the shops together to choose it. My, it was hot in Pompeii this morning. I could feel the heat rise through the soles of my sandals. Three times we stopped at the public fountains to drink. The colonnades were crowded with people sheltering from the sun.

We wandered slowly up and down the street. Mother usually enjoys shopping. I do not! But surely no one could enjoy shopping today. To make matters worse, every few yards we had to stop – some fabric to admire or a friend to hail.

At home again I tried on my new tunic. Mother pinned brooches to my shoulders to hold the gown in place. It reaches right to my toes. Do they want to hobble me?

"How grown-up you look, Claudia," Mother said, sounding pleased. I do not care to be grown up, so I took the mirror Mother handed me most reluctantly. Anyway, it will take more than a new tunic to make me feel grown-up inside.

18 September

I am writing this curled up on my bed – back in my old tunic, every trace of make-up scrubbed from my face. It feels red and sore, but at least I look like Claudia again, even if inside I still feel most uncomfortable.

I had to wear my new tunic today. I do not know how I managed not to trip and tear it, but I wish I had. Then perhaps Quintus would not have stared at me.

We had been invited to dine at Vastus's home in honour of his new bakery. What a fuss Mother made. You'd have thought we'd been invited to dine with the emperor.

My lips were dabbed with red ochre, my eyebrows darkened with a concoction that smelled as if it had been scooped straight out of the brazier, my hair tugged and pulled and curled with Mother's tongs. Father looked at me as if he hardly knew me. I confess I hardly knew myself.

Vastus's home is just a short walk from ours. A good thing too – I could barely shuffle in my new tunic and sandals.

At the entrance to the house, a slave barred our way. He looked us up and down, and I swear his lip curled. He ushered us through into the shady atrium, where we were greeted by Vastus and Pompeia. I could not stop myself from staring at Pompeia's hair. Each time I see it, it is a different colour. Today it was blonde.

"Why, Claudia, you do look pretty," Aemilia said, smiling and drawing my arm through hers. I simpered back. I felt like a dressed-up doll, so I'd behave like one. We walked together into the garden.

Aemilia is very proud of their home. And every time I visit there is something new to admire. A newly laid mosaic floor, or a statue maybe. I wondered what she'd show me today.

I confess I do like their courtyard garden. They have a fig tree like us and roses climb up the colonnades. The roses grow plentifully, even in summer, for they are well watered by the fountains. The family doesn't rely on a well or the public fountains for their water like us. Their water is piped into the house.

We gathered in the shade under the colonnades. "Why! A water clock," Father said, bending down to look at something. A water clock tells the time, Father told me – just like our sundial. He showed me how it worked. You fill a vessel with water, and as it escapes it shows you the hour. And unlike our sundial, which can only show you the hour of the day,

41

and then only when the sun is shining, it tells the time both day and night. Vastus says it is much more reliable than the sundial, but this one certainly isn't.

The tenth hour it declared, and we all knew it was only the fifth – for that's the hour at which we dine.

We were led into the dining room. While slaves washed our feet I looked round the room. My, it is grand. Paintings of fat men and women eating and drinking – Aemilia says they are gods – run round the walls. Couches had been placed round three sides of the big table. The table itself was decorated with mosaics – I picked out bunches of grapes, fish and flagons.

Lunch itself was a dreary business. How grown-ups like to talk! By listening you learn, Father always says, but how much can you learn about a new bakery? Quintus will run it, Vastus told us. He's very proud of his son – and I am sure that Quintus shares his father's high opinion of him. Every time Vastus praised him – which was often – he smirked and tried to catch my eye. I think my made-up face had caught his fancy. I withdrew my eyes hastily. He has not caught mine! But at least he doesn't spatter you when he eats like his younger brother Gaius.

And my, what a lot there was to eat! We have a simple meal at this time of day, but their table was laden as for a banquet. Bronze and silver platters crammed with all manner of meats and fish, fruits and cheeses. Just looking at it made me feel sick. No wonder Vastus is so fat.

First, there were stuffed dormice. Vastus rubbed his hands gleefully, as slaves brought these to the table. Stuffed dormice are a great delicacy, but they make Father belch. I dropped mine, half-eaten, on the floor, and pushed it away under the couch with my foot. Mother chewed and chewed – her face growing a faint greenish colour as Quintus described how they'd been stuffed and sewn up again. I yearned to kick him.

"Isn't Quintus handsome?" Aemilia whispered to me afterwards. I muttered something to please her, though how even a fond sister can think such a long-faced fellow handsome I cannot imagine. And the way he looked at me turned my stomach.

Quintus led the way to the new bakery. I loitered as far back in the party as I could, feeling as fat and full as one of those stuffed dormice.

Like ours, Vastus's new bakery has been built out of a once-grand house, but everything else about it is new and of the finest quality, from the shop counter to the millstone.

Oh, that millstone! It was awful! Father had his back to it, talking to Quintus, but when he turned and saw it, he fell silent. Two boys were turning it. Boys – yoked like donkeys to the paddle, their backs gleaming with sweat. One of the two glanced up at us – eyes sullen. His hair was no longer matted and he wore a clean loincloth, but I recognized him at once. It was the boy Vastus had bought at the slave auction.

And then something rang in my memory. The fair

skin. That reddish hair. Where had I seen it before? Then I remembered. The girl at the laundry. The girl scowling in the slave market. They were one and the same. His sister. It must be. How many people in Pompeii have hair and skin like that? The boy did not look at us again, as he toiled round, head bent low.

Father looked grim. "It is hard work for two lads," he murmured to Vastus.

Vastus grunted. "Aye, it will teach them not to misbehave."

"It is a punishment, then," Father said, and I could hear the slight question in his voice. Mother looked stricken.

"Aye," said Vastus, impatiently, as if he'd had enough questioning. He slapped Father's shoulder. "Quintus has suggested a new line – sacrificial flour for the temples. What do you say to that?" He looked proudly at his son.

I turned away. I could not bear to gawp at those poor boys.

Quintus glanced at me. He went up to his father and murmured something. "Aye, aye," Vastus said. "Stop the mill!"

The mill was stopped and the boys released. They leant over the paddles, breathing heavily, as if too exhausted to move.

Quintus suggested a tour of the bakery. So we gazed politely at the oven and admired its chimney. Then to the stables. The two donkeys there looked quite content – as well they might. It had been a day of rest for them.

But I felt far from content. I had an uneasy feeling that the mill had been stopped merely to please me. And – until we departed – Quintus stuck like a leech to my side. I saw Father smile, as if the sight pleased him. It did not please me.

I glanced back as we left the bakery. But the barbarian boy had gone.

OCTOBRIS
1 October

I am lying on one elbow, my ankle propped up. It is most uncomfortable but it is the only position I can write in. My ankle still looks huge, in spite of the ointment Mother has rubbed on it. And it throbs. How it throbs. But worse – far worse – someone may have been punished, and all because of me.

I do not know how long I lay there, feeling miserable and wishing I had some way to give vent to my feelings. Mother told me I was to reflect on my behaviour. I have had plenty of time to reflect now. And I do not like it. Heedless, she called me. Unthinking. It was dark long before Fausta came to light the lamp by my bed. I do not like the dark. I watched as she filled the lamp with olive oil and trimmed the wick. She said not a word to me.

It was only after Fausta had left that I remembered you. Dear diary. How could I have forgotten you? You are such a comfort to me. But it was a long slow hop to the chest and I had to rummage through it with one hand, while clinging to the edge with the other. I still cannot put any weight on my foot.

Now – where do I begin? Where did it all go wrong?

This afternoon, at the bakery.

I'd gone to see Pollux. I hadn't planned to take him out, but he looked at me so mournfully. Before I knew what I was doing I'd unchained him. He darted eagerly forward. "Just a short walk then," I thought, hastening after him.

I turned off the main street and stopped. Ahead of me were the big stones that we use to cross the street to avoid stepping in the filth and water below. Suddenly I had such an urge to jump them. It was a game I used to play. The last time I'd done this I'd barely managed one. But my legs are longer now. I looked round. It was late in the afternoon, and the street was empty. It was now, or never. I looped Pollux's chain over a stone. Then I hitched up my tunic and leaped as far as I could. My foot brushed the edge of a stone – and down I tumbled, my ankle twisted under me.

How it hurt. I tried to stand, but pain shot through my foot, and I sank back down again. Except for Pollux and the chatter of the mosquitoes the street was quiet. How long would I have to lie there before anyone came to help me?

But who would come? How often Fausta had warned me of the spirits that haunt the city at dusk, ready to snatch up abandoned children. And the sun was low now – those spirits would be abroad. Bad people too, loiter the streets of Pompeii. I could not lie there – somehow I had to make my own way home. I would have to crawl to the stone where Pollux was tied, and use that to help myself up. Then hop home somehow. I looked at the street. It was filthy. My tunic was already dirtied from my fall, but it would be much filthier by the time I'd crawled across the street. Mother would be so angry.

I burst into tears. How foolish I'd been.

Suddenly I froze. Pollux had been barking his head off but now he began to growl. Someone or some *thing* was running down the street.

I could hear hurried breathing as the steps grew nearer. They stopped.

Help was at hand – or was it? Would whoever or whatever it was aid me – or hurt me?

In terror I screwed up my eyes. "Isis, protect me," I whispered.

Cautiously, I opened my eyes, one after the other.

A boy was crouching next to me. I could see from the disc he wore that he was a slave. I recognized him at once. I'd last seen him turning the millstone in Vastus's new bakery. Oh, the relief! On the ground next to me was a basket of loaves. It looked half-empty. I glanced back. Three or four loaves had spilled out. He must have dropped them when he ran to my aid.

Then, with a shock I realized he had no idea who I was. I shrank back – afraid again. I remembered what I'd heard about the Britons. How few respected them. That they were woad-painted savages – always drinking and fighting.

"Don't be afraid," the boy said. "I won't hurt you." He spoke my language, but the accent was a strange one.

"Are you badly hurt?" he asked.

"It's my ankle," I said. "I think I've twisted it."

He bent down. "Can I look at it?" he said.

I nodded shyly, wincing as he gently felt it. "It is twisted," he said. "No bones broken. Try to stand." He held out his hand encouragingly. "I'll help you." I took his hand and he pulled me to my feet. But oh my. How it hurt.

Pollux was still growling. "Is that your dog?" the boy asked. I nodded and the boy smiled. "I'm sure I've seen him before," he said, wrinkling his forehead, as if striving to remember where. Now, I thought, now he'd remember me. But he didn't – and after a moment's thought actually I was glad. Did I want him to remember that dressed-up girl who'd gawped at him in the bakery, the girl who'd pulled Pollux away from him at the slave market? No, I did not! The boy seemed to have forgotten me. He held out his hand to Pollux. "Aiee," he called softly. "Aiee." Then the most extraordinary thing happened. Pollux stopped growling! The boy helped me over the street, but his eyes were still fixed on Pollux. He crouched down next to him while I propped myself up against a wall. I heard him murmur something. I could not understand what he was saying, but I am sure that Pollux did.

He nuzzled his head into the boy's hand – just as he had at the slave market.

"I like your dog," the boy said. He wrapped Pollux's chain round his wrist. "Come," he said, gently pulling the chain. Pollux looked questioningly at me, but for once he did as he was told.

At the entrance to my home, the boy left me. "You will be all right now," he said. I thanked him, holding out my hand. He took it but dropped it almost at once. "I must go," he said, nervously backing away. I watched as he ran away down the street.

Mother was beside herself with worry. "How could you think of running off like that?" she exclaimed. "Do you not know how worried we were? Child, what if the spirits had come for you – alone and unprotected as you were." Then she saw my dirty tunic, and began to scold me. She ordered me to my room but as soon as I tried to put weight on my foot, pain shot up my ankle again. "How did you come to hurt it?" she asked me, rubbing a salve of meadowsweet and pig's fat on it. I blushed but I told her the truth. "Foolish child," she scolded. "You are too old for such games."

She asked how I'd got myself home – barely able to walk as I am. "A boy helped me," I said. Then I remembered something. His loaves. He'd forgotten them! Someone would surely have stolen them by now.

"He left his basket of loaves in the street," I said. "I'm afraid he'll be punished for that."

Mother sighed. "Poor lad," she said. And then she talked to me, so seriously that I cried. She reminded me of the duties expected of a Roman girl. Obedience. Respect. Discipline. Dignity. Cleanliness. Tidiness. Politeness. How long the list seemed. How much longer the list of my failures.

I thought Father would beat me but he says the pain is punishment enough. He looked sternly at me. "Child, I trust the hurt will teach you what we cannot," he said.

3 October

My ankle still throbs and I can barely hobble. Mother's ointment has not helped at all. And this afternoon I was punished further.

Aemilia came to visit me, and I had to endure an hour of silly gossip. After she'd left she promised to return soon. My heart sank. "And when your ankle has mended, you must come and visit me," she said, giving me a sidelong glance. I felt certain she had Quintus in her thoughts. I am sure she wants to bring us together as much as I want to keep us apart.

I was happier to see Marcus and Sextus. We played for a time with my marbles, but then Mother saw them and shooed them away, and I have had nothing to do since but lie and stare at the ceiling. I think Mother is pleased that I am stuck here – so bored and restless.

7 October

The swelling on my ankle has gone down, and this morning when Mother touched it, I barely winced at all. I'd hoped it would let me off spinning and weaving, but Mother says if you can hop to the dining room, you can hop to the weaving loom too.

Stuck here in the house, I cannot escape from Aemilia's visits. I have had *three* since I hurt my ankle. Mother says it is kind of her, but she does not have to listen to her. Yesterday I nearly lost my temper. Why are girls so silly! Why do they talk about boys all the time? Aemilia has told me that her friend Iunia is betrothed. Her betrothed is rich, but old, she says – a man of forty. She is but thirteen. Poor Iunia. I would not like to marry a man as old as that.

8 October

Claudia, you are a selfish girl. You think only of your own problems. Heedless, Mother called me. Unthinking. She is right. I had forgotten all about that poor boy. What if he's been punished? It would be all my fault. So I have made up my mind. When I next see Aemilia, I will try to find out.

Father says he is pleased how bravely I have borne my hurt. I am glad that there is something about me he can be proud of. But alone I grit my teeth. I am angry with them – and myself. Why do I find it so hard to be a good and obedient Roman girl?

14 October

Aemilia was at the baths today.

"Now that your ankle has mended you can come and visit me," she said, smiling as she took my arm. I took a deep breath, my heart thumping. Now – now I could find out if that boy had been punished.

"I have something to ask you," I said. To my annoyance I felt myself blush. Aemilia smiled, and squeezed my arm. I felt my cheeks grow hotter still. Why must she smile at me like that? I pressed on. I had to explain now. I could not let her think that I was moping over her brother.

I told her that a boy had helped me home after my accident. "He is a slave in your new bakery," I said. "He was turning the millstone when we came to see it. He may have been punished for helping me when he should have been delivering the bread. But he shouldn't have been punished. He only stopped to help me." I stopped, confused.

Aemilia was looking at me, as if I was mad.

"All this fuss – about a slave," she said.

"Slave or not, he should not be punished," I said stubbornly.

"Which of the two was it?" Aemilia asked.

"The Briton," I said. Aemilia giggled, shocked. "Claudia – a Briton," she squeaked. "They're barbarians! And, then – *that* boy! He's rough, sullen, and dirty!"

And it was she who'd said he was handsome! Did she think *I* had a fancy for him? I felt myself flush again – angrily this time. A long strand of her hair had come loose. I longed to pull it.

"He was kind and he helped me. That is all," I said, crossly. But all Aemilia would say was that her brother would never punish a slave unless he deserved it. I am sure he has been punished even so. Quintus is quite mean enough. I wish now that I had said nothing at all.

NOVEMBRIS
6 November

We are weaving blankets, ready for winter. The nights are growing cooler now, and we have need of them.

I began mine a few days ago and have made some little progress. But my, won't I be glad when I can sit down to weave. The top of the loom is too high for me to reach, unless I stand on a stool. By the end of the morning my arms and legs are aching.

Mother says my cloth is as well made as the cloth from Britain! British cloth is very fine, Mother says, so I think she says it merely to encourage me. Mother favours their red woollen cloth most of all – but it is costly.

That started me thinking. If the Britons are such savages, how is it they make such fine woollen cloth? They are good horsemen and love animals, too – as I have discovered. I am beginning to think that many of the stories circulated about the Britons must be false.

I have not seen the British boy since the day I hurt my ankle. But then I have done my best to avoid the bakery for fear of meeting that odious Quintus.

Father has given me another scroll. "You may find a use for this," he told me. I know I shall!

15 November

I have seen the British boy again. And I am sad. But I will come to that later.

It was at the Forum, where Mother had sent me to buy fish. I nearly walked straight into him. My mind was busy. Would Mother like my fish? I was wondering. Was it truly fresh? "Check the fish's eyes," she had told me. "If they are dull, it is not fresh. Ask for Primus. You can trust him." I must have looked worried for she had added: "Xenia will help you."

But Xenia did not!

Somewhere among the Forum crowds we had lost each other. So I walked boldly on alone through the vast entrance to the Macellum to where fish is displayed on a large marble counter. A fountain sprays cold water over it to keep it fresh. All around me were men, gutting and scaling fish, tossing the unwanted bits into the stone gutter. How curiously they stared at me. What have we here? A rich girl, unattended. I sped to the counter. I would buy my fish, and leave – fast.

I asked for Primus loudly. Three men looked up – each

claiming to be Primus. I looked helplessly from one to the other. Surely they weren't all called Primus? One of the three picked up a fish and waved it at me. It looked slimy and it stank. I couldn't trust him.

What had Mother said? "If the eyes are dull, it is not fresh." My hand hovered over the counter.

"I'll take this," I said pointing at a clear-eyed fat fish. Primus 2 told me it was his.

Primus 3 spat. "It is not yours to sell – son of a thief!" Primus 2 looked so angry I thought he'd hit him! By the time they'd stopped arguing and the fish had been boned and wrapped I felt as limp as the fish. Meanwhile, where was Xenia?

I passed the holitorium, where the grain is sold. And it was there that I saw the British boy. He was bent low, a sack of grain over one shoulder. He glanced up as I hastily stepped aside and smiled. He asked if my ankle was mended, and I if he'd been punished. He grimaced and nodded. I did feel awful. I told him I was sorry. He put down the sack.

"Where's your dog?" he asked.

I told him I'd left him at home. "Sometimes he runs off," I said, "especially on market days."

The boy half-smiled. At home in Britain, he said, they'd had dogs and horses. His father had driven a chariot. He'd taught him to drive it too. "There is nothing in the world like it," he said dreamily. He stared into the distance as if he'd forgotten where he was, as if he was far away, standing next to his father in his chariot again, hair flying out behind him, horses' hooves thundering, the dogs running alongside. Then he looked down, scuffing the ground with his foot. I felt so sorry for him. What a fine life he'd lost.

I sought to find something to say. "You speak Latin well," I said. "How did you come to learn it?"

As soon as I'd spoken I could have bitten off my tongue. What a stupid thing to say.

The boy scowled at me – all friendliness gone.

"How do you think I learned it? You Romans invaded my land – and stole my father's chariot. Now my father and mother lie dead and my sister and I are slaves."

He spat. "I hate all Romans. And here I am talking to a rich Roman girl."

I bridled. "My father and mother were slaves once too," I said tartly. "If their master hadn't freed them, I'd be a slave now, like you."

He looked surprised.

"You may not always be a slave either," I said gently.

People were shoving past us and I could feel blood leak from the fish. I could not linger long. Nor could he – or he'd be in trouble again.

"You are right," he said at last. "I will not always be a slave. As soon as I find my sister, I will leave this accursed town."

"What – run away!" I exclaimed. "You'll be brought back and punished – branded here" – I pressed my hand to my forehead – "maybe even put to death." The boy said nothing, but hoisted the sack up on to his back. I followed him through the crowds. He had a fast stride and I could barely keep up. At the top of the Forum steps he stopped to push a lock of hair back off his face.

"Do not run away," I said, breathlessly, as I caught up with him. "Please."

"Why should you care, Roman girl," he said.

"Because you were kind and helped me," I said.

"I'd help any poor creature that hurt itself – man or dog," he said.

He spoke so rudely that I lost my temper. "Run then," I said angrily. "And pay the penalty. You'll surely be caught."

He laughed. "You have spirit, Roman girl."

Still laughing, he bounded down the steps, as if the sack was no heavier than a baby. I followed as fast as I could, tripping down the steps after him. Angry though I was, I had something more to say. Something important. But before I was even halfway down, I could hear Xenia's voice, calling my name. If I did not speak soon, it would be too late.

So I did something a well brought up Roman girl should never do. I cupped my hands to my mouth and bawled like any fish-seller: "Ask at the laundry of Stephanus. You'll find your sister there." People turned their heads to stare at me. But was his amongst them? I could not tell.

All flustered, Xenia burst down the steps. "Oh, young

58

mistress," she said, her voice trembling. "Oh, young mistress."

"Do not fret," I told her. "I am safe. I will not tell Mother that you lost me."

And I will not. But how I wish I could tell Marcus about that young charioteer. How he would love to talk to him. But it can never be.

I felt sad and then I remembered how rude he'd been. He hates us Romans. And – thinking about it now – I am sure I'd hate us too if I were him.

18 November

I am bored bored bored. It is wet outside, so I cannot even take Pollux out for a walk. Mother says I spend too much time dawdling around the kitchen, and disturbing the slaves at their work. If you're not upsetting them, you are hiding in your room, she says. What do you do in there all the time on your own?

If you have nothing better to do, she said next, please will you finish your blanket.

This afternoon some of Mother's friends came to call. I listened to their chatter, wishing I had someone to talk to. I have my diary but it cannot talk to me. I love Pollux dearly, but he cannot talk either. If only I had a friend – a proper friend. Someone I could share secrets with, someone who is not too grown-up to run and jump and play. Aemilia was kind to me when I hurt my ankle, but we have little to say to each other. Little we can share.

20 November

Pollux ran away today. My, I was upset. Mother said it was good riddance. He is a useless guard dog, she said. Samius does not look after him properly, I cried. He is often hungry and thirsty. Is it his fault he runs? He is a greedy dog, Mother said firmly.

I could not settle. Each time I thought I heard a dog bark, I started. Finally, Mother sighed and told me I might go round to the bakery to see if he had returned. "But mind you come straight back," she said. "I do not want to lose you too."

I searched for Pollux everywhere. I even went into the stable where the millstone donkeys are tethered. Pollux likes to forage there. But there was no sign of him there either. Then I saw that the side gate had swung open. I slipped out. I wouldn't go far, I promised myself. Just along the street.

Outside, the din hit me like a blacksmith's hammer.

I despaired. How ever would I find him? How would I hear his bark?

At Vastus's new bakery I hesitated. I was about to scuttle past – for fear of seeing Quintus – when a big man lurched out of the entrance. "Mind yourself," he growled, rudely shoving past me. His breath reeked of garlic. Faugh! He did not look at me, but I'd have known that scarred and angry face anywhere. It was the gladiators' trainer. What, I wondered, was he doing there?

But Pollux was nowhere to be seen. Sadly, I wended my way home. I was almost back when I heard a bark. I knew that bark. Quickly I turned round.

A bedraggled Pollux leaped for my lap, trailing his chain behind him. His ear was torn. He whimpered plaintively as I touched it.

"Oh, Pollux! How did you hurt your ear?" I cried, cuddling him.

"It got caught in another dog's teeth," a voice laughed. I looked up to see the barbarian boy. I was so surprised that I just crouched there, gaping at him.

"Where did you find him?" I asked at last, nervously – remembering the unfriendly manner in which we'd parted in the Forum.

"At the Nucerian Gate," the boy said.

"The Nucerian Gate!" I exclaimed. What had made Pollux run so far? And to that place, of all places! And what had *he*

61

been doing there? The Nucerian Gate leads to the City of the Dead. It's a terrible place. Only wraiths and spirits dare to linger there.

The boy pushed back his hair and I saw the scratches on his hands and arms. He must have hurt them pulling the dogs apart.

I pushed Pollux off. "Why must you fight? Why run away? You'll get no sympathy from me," I scolded.

I wound his chain around my hand and stood up.

Only then did I see my tunic. Oh my! There were paw prints all over it. If Mother saw it I'd be in trouble again. Hastily I waved farewell to the boy and ran, Pollux bounding ahead of me.

I rinsed my tunic under a fountain. It was still damp and rumpled when I got home so I changed it quickly before Mother saw me. I told her that I had found Pollux. In spite of what she'd said, she seemed pleased.

21 November

I have a secret. It is a secret SO big that I almost dare not write it, even in my diary. So all I will say is that I have made a friend. I think I can call him that – though I do not know him well – for he has told me his name. Not his slave name, Rufus, which means reddish in my language – reddish like his hair – but his true name. Aengus. The name given him by his people. It is a big thing to be so trusted.

I had just left our bakery, when I saw him – my new friend – loitering in the street outside our house. I could not think what he was doing there, but he smiled when he saw me.

"I have something to say to you," he whispered.

"Follow me," I whispered back. "It is not safe to talk here." We turned off the main street, me glancing back hastily in case anyone saw us.

"I came to thank you," he said. "I would have thanked you yesterday but you ran away."

I was puzzled. What did he have to thank me for? He found my dog. Surely I should thank him.

"You told me where I might find my sister," he explained.

"Did you find her? Was she at the laundry?" I asked eagerly.

He shook his head disconsolately. "No. They have turned her away. Maybe they found out that she is left-handed. I am told you think it is unlucky. But I will not give up – not yet." He smiled at me. "You tried to help me – even though I was rude to you. I am grateful. Few Romans have shown me any kindness."

I saw then that his arms and legs were bruised as well as scratched. I'm sure all he finds in Quintus's bakery are beatings and cruel words.

Aengus was staring at Vesuvius. "I am afraid of that mountain," he said suddenly. "I think it harbours something bad. When the ground shook, I thought there is something there – inside that mountain – that causes the ground to shake. Is it one of your gods?" I shook my head, but uncertainly, my thoughts all in a whirl. How strange that he should think that.

28 November

Lightning flashed across the sky from left to right today. THAT IS A VERY BAD PORTENT.

"What does it mean?" Marcus asked Sextus and me. We three were standing in the atrium, looking up at the sky, which had grown as dark as night.

"I don't know," I said nervously.

Marcus wanted to toss the knucklebones again. But I would not. So he sulked and took Sextus away to play with them. And now they will not tell me what they said. It is a secret, Marcus said importantly – as if the whole mystery of the universe had been revealed to them in one throw of the knucklebones. But he looked scared. They are just stupid.

DECEMBRIS
1 December

Ancient was at the market today. When Mother's back was turned, I sidled up to him. The lightning and Aengus's words about Vesuvius had troubled me. I had to speak to someone – someone like Ancient who understood what others did not. But I am little the wiser now. Watch, he said to me. Listen.

He was sitting in his usual place, hunched up by a stall, his lame leg tucked under him. I opened my mouth to greet him and then I shut it again. Now that I could speak, I did not know what to say.

"You said that Vulcan was angry," I blurted out at last.

Ancient turned his old eyes on me. They looked half-blind like Fausta's. "It is a strange way to greet an old man, child." I flushed. "I am sorry, Ancient one," I said humbly. "But," I drew a deep breath, "I heard what you said in the Forum, the day the ground shook. That was a portent, I know, and there have been many portents since. I am afraid..." My voice tailed away. I looked at Ancient. He was eating a pie, and crumbs dripped from his chin. "You said that Vulcan was angry," I persisted. "That he'd sent us a warning."

"Aye," he said. "I said it – and I would say it again."

I swallowed. If only he hadn't said that. If only I hadn't begun such a conversation. "Will there be another great earthquake? Is that what Vulcan's warning means?" I got out at last, my voice barely more than a whisper. "Will our city be destroyed again?" a little voice added in my head.

Ancient wiped his hand across his mouth and tapped his eyes – first the left one, and then the right. "You see these old eyes of mine? I do not see well with them now, but I can still hear. I listen, child. I listen. The world abounds with signs for those who learn to look and listen.

"I have heard of stars on fire falling from the heavens, hissing like red-hot iron plunged into cold water. Of lightning that forks the sky from left to right," he said. I swallowed again, my mouth as dry as sand. My brothers and I had seen that lightning. "Some say that these are portents, others that they are Nature's signs. Call them what you will. Observe these signs, child, if you wish to understand what the gods have in store for us."

3 December

We have met several times now – Aengus and me. We usually meet at the end of the day, near our bakery. I slip out of the side gate when I hear his signal – an owl-hoot. Aengus is trying to teach me to hoot so I can send him messages too. I purse up my lips as he shows me and blow. But all that comes out is a lot of breath. That makes him laugh. It is good to hear Aengus laugh – he can have precious little to laugh about, a slave in Quintus's bakery. I suggested we write messages on the wall instead. In code, so that no one but us could read them. But Aengus cannot read or write.

He would like us to meet further away. He is afraid that someone will see us, as am I. But I told him that then I would have a slave tailing behind me. I can rarely go out on my own. It is not safe, I say. I am good with my fists, he says. I will look after you. I like to hear him say that. Sometimes I wonder why I like him so much. Is it because he listens to me? And I can be myself with Aengus. I do not have to pretend to be grown-up, or a good and proper Roman girl.

I bring Pollux with me as often as I can, for I am sure it is really Pollux Aengus wants to see. And Pollux loves that boy – almost as much as he loves me I think. When he sees him he jumps up and licks his face and hands all over. I feel quite jealous!

12 December

We are preparing for the great festival of Saturnalia. The slaves are cooking and the whole house smells of spices. Xenia says it reminds her of her homeland. A hot and spicy place that must be.

Here, it is not hot. It is grey and wet. So we went by litter to the baths. I did feel grand. But riding in a litter is not always comfortable. On the way back, I nearly toppled out when my litter lurched to avoid a child. As I pulled myself back up, I glanced through the curtains. Water was trickling down the slaves' backs and they were up to their ankles in mud and rubbish. What must it be like to live in a country like Britain? It rains all the time there, I'm told.

13 December

Aengus's appetite is even bigger than mine. He is always hungry. I filch food when I can from the kitchen or the table, hiding it in my tunic. Mother is puzzled by the size of my appetite these days. "Where do you put it all?" she asks. "You have not grown any fatter."

Poor Aengus. It is rare to see him without some hurt. Ianuarius, the bakery foreman, is a cruel man, he tells me. He beats him often, and calls him a "dirty Briton". Sometimes he even tries to trip him up, and then Aengus is punished for that! And the master does nothing to stop him. I can well believe it. I nearly said so too, but I stopped myself just in time. I do not want Aengus to learn about my family's friendship with his master's. I fear he would never speak to me again.

17 December

My lamp has gone out, but I have opened the shutters a crack so I can see by the glow from the torches in the street below. At the end of my bed Fausta's snores tell me that she is sleeping soundly. I wonder that she can. The shops are closed for the festival but the taverns are doing a roaring trade. Fortunes are being won and lost in those taverns. It is only during Saturnalia that gambling is allowed – though I don't think many heed the law. "Io Saturnalia. Io Saturnalia! Hail Saturnalia!" people bawl, tramping up and down. On our way back from the temple I spotted Samius rolling down the street, his face shining red in the torch-light, his freedman's cap askew over one ear. Everyone dons the freedman's cap during Saturnalia, so you cannot tell who is a slave, or who free. Slaves become masters and masters slaves. It is most confusing!

Saturnalia is my favourite festival. It begins solemnly enough, with a ceremony to honour Saturn, the god of sowing. We watched as the priests loosened the bindings that fastened the god's ankles.

"Why do they do this?" Sextus asked as he always does.

"It is a symbol," Father said.

"Of what?" Sextus wanted to know.

"Of the mayhem about to begin," Father said solemnly, but his eyes were twinkling so I know that he was teasing. On our way back, we passed Quintus's bakery. I glanced in quickly, but I couldn't see Aengus.

Uncle arrived last night, bringing olives for us, and a goat for the sacrifice. A more bad-tempered goat I have never seen. It spent its last night in the bakery stables, tethered far from the donkeys in case it kicked them. I think it knew its fate, for this morning it did its best to kick me.

After the goat is sacrificed, part is left to be eaten by the god and the priests. We feasted on what was left. Uncle popped in and out of the kitchen all through its cooking. Was the oven hot enough? Were more herbs needed? Fausta's murmurs grew louder.

"Doesn't Uncle know that it is on the last day of the festival that masters serve the slaves?" Marcus muttered to me.

We drew lots to see who would be King of Saturnalia this year. Everyone takes part – even the slaves. The king becomes master of the household for one day. Chius blushed scarlet when his name was drawn. Chius is so shy. I cannot imagine him ordering anyone about.

20 December

Just one thing spoils the festival for me. We are to dine at Vastus's house in three days' time. I will have my face made up, be pulled into my best tunic and – oh Isis! – have to be polite to Quintus. The thought makes me feel quite ill.

24 December

Here in my room I can still hear the laughter. The revels are not yet over. I crept away early pleading that I was sleepy. In truth, I was feeling a bit sick.

We waited on the slaves at dinner. Father served the wine. He is quite subdued today. How surprised he was to learn of Quintus's betrothal to Iulia.

"My dear child," he said to me. "Are you very disappointed?" I nearly choked on my honeycake.

Disappointed! Me! Why, when Aemilia told me I had to fight to stop a grin spreading over my face.

"Quintus is betrothed," she whispered, drawing me away from everyone else. Iulia is the daughter of one of the richest bakers in Pompeii.

She told me she wished Quintus was marrying me. "We could have been sisters," she said. She looked sad, and so I tried to pull a sad look on to my face too. But inside I was singing and dancing. No longer would I have to endure Quintus's loathsome attentions.

I still feel sick. Mother says I deserve to be. We had snails *and* honeycakes for dinner. I don't care for snails – but I ate four honeycakes.

Well, at least I am not as greedy as Gaius. He had six yesterday. I counted.

KALENDS – I IANUARIUS AD 79
SCROLL THE SECOND

I have begun the second scroll. It is a good time to do so – the beginning of a new year.

As is our custom we went to the Temple to thank Jupiter for looking after us in the old year and to ask for his protection in the new. There were so many people there, pressing forward to see the ceremony, that I could see little of it. Nor hear much either. Behind the temple I could see the great bulk of Vesuvius. I am trying my best to forget how it frightened me last year. But how big it is. How tiny and unimportant we seem next to it.

3 January

I am discovering more about Britain. Aengus lived in the north of the country – a wild land much of which is still unconquered.

His father died in a raiding party, he told me. He was betrayed by one of his brothers. How awful – to be betrayed by your own brother. Aengus does not often talk about his family. I think it hurts him too much. I told him that Mother has not seen any of her brothers and sisters since she was a child. As soon as I'd said that, I wished I hadn't. Aengus looked so sad. I felt sure he was thinking about his sister. He has still not found her. So I told him that Father has a brother that he sees often. And that Mother was born in Egypt – so of course she would not see her family. That is not the whole truth, but it cheered him a little. And I think he is glad to know that I am not of solid Roman stock. It is a bond between us.

Aengus is teaching me about animals. "They are cleverer than us in many ways. Look how he listens," he said as Pollux cocked his ears. "He can hear things we cannot. He can sense if something is wrong. We should pay close heed to the animals. We can learn much from them." I remembered what Ancient had said to me in the Forum – words I'd sooner forget. Take heed of Nature's signs, he had told me, if you wish to know what the gods have in store for you. Hastily I asked Aengus to tell me instead about the chariot races they hold in his homeland.

"The British chariots can hold two men," he said. "In battle, one steers the horses, the other fights. Sometimes, the warrior jumps down on to the pole to fight, or leaps off the chariot altogether." He showed me how they use the reins to steer the horses. "But a good horseman is guided by his horse too," he said.

I am saving up everything Aengus tells me. Perhaps one day I'll be able to tell Marcus.

8 January

Mother says I daydream too much. "What is the matter with you, Claudia? You do not attend to what I say. It is like getting wool from an ass," she says despairingly.

Marcus says I am all mopey. "I do not mope," I told him haughtily. He looked at me – a long and suspicious look. For one horrible moment I feared that he had guessed my secret. Has he seen me slip out to meet Aengus? He *can't* have.

I have seen Quintus's betrothed. Her face is as long as a donkey's. They suit each other.

10 January

Such luck! I found a cast-off snakeskin outside yesterday. Snakes bring good fortune so I put it away in my chest with my other special treasures, but a bit broke off. I did not like to throw it away – that would be unlucky – so I sat wondering what to do with it. Suddenly I had such a brilliant idea. With the end of my stylus I scraped some wax off my tablet and pressed the bit of snakeskin deep into it. I shaped the wax into a little round – rather as if I was making a loaf of bread. Then I threaded a leather thong through one end and tied it in a knot. There! I had made a bulla. Tomorrow, I will give it to Aengus. I hope it will bring him good fortune. Maybe it will help him find his sister. I hope he does – and yet I hope he does not. Is that very selfish of me? But I am afraid they will run away together if he finds her, and I am sure they'll be caught and terribly punished if they do.

11 January

It is such fun having a secret friend. Today I gave Aengus the bulla I'd made for him. "What is this?" he said shyly, looking at the thing in his hand.

"It is a bulla – a good luck charm," I said. He swung the charm on its leather thong. "It is to protect you from evil," I added. "See, there is a bit of snakeskin in it. That should bring you good fortune."

"Where did you get it?" he asked.

"I made it myself," I said, trying to keep the pride out of my voice.

"Then I will value it all the more," he said. I did feel pleased!

"Wear it under your tunic," I told him. "Then no one will see it."

I watched as he slipped it over his neck. "I wish I had something for you," he said sadly. "All I can give you is my friendship, Claudia."

"All," I said. "That is a very big thing." And then I made a solemn promise. "I will never betray it," I told him. "Never."

13 January

Aengus has a black eye, but he will not tell me how he got it. I suspect Ianuarius gave it to him. I got Fausta to make me a potion for it. She did not ask why I wanted it, but her clouded eye seemed to look deep into me. I felt myself blush. I have not told her about my new friend, of course. I have not told anyone about him. But Fausta can see things that others do not. Has she guessed my secret?

15 January

Father has seen the lanista – at Vastus's house! I could hear in Father's voice how surprised he was. Gladiators are not at all respectable people. Why is such a man hanging around Vastus's house? The answer came straight back to me – in Father's own words. He still hopes to buy that boy.

Anyway, what other reason could there be?

Aengus is often put to work the millstone. Turning it will build up his strength. (As does the food I take him.) Vastus will get a fat price for him if he sells him now.

Should I warn Aengus? But if I do, he may run away. He is hot-headed enough. And what if Father is wrong? Oh, if only I knew what to do. How awful to be a slave – just something to be bought or sold at your master's will.

17 January

I have had such a fright. I had just given Aengus the potion Fausta had made for me, when I heard a voice call my name.

I jumped. Oh Isis! It was Aemilia!

"Go!" I hissed to Aengus. "Make haste!" Aengus disappeared round the corner of the house and I turned round slowly. Aemilia was arm in arm with a girl I had never seen before.

"Why, Aemilia," I said, as nonchalantly as I could, but my heart was beating heavily.

"Who were you talking to, Claudia?" she asked curiously.

I floundered. Would I were as quick with my tongue as I am with my pen!

"Me? No one," I said at last, as coolly as I could.

Aemilia looked doubtful.

"I was going over some numbers in my head. I help Father with his letters, sometimes," I added hastily. Aemilia shrugged, and I flushed. It had been a stupid thing to say.

"Farewell, Claudia," she said stiffly. I watched them walk away, my heart still thumping.

Did they see Aengus? Did they? I cannot believe how stupid we've been. Claudia, in future, you must take more care.

20 January

I have made a new friend. Her name is Calpurnia and she is Aemilia's cousin! How could two such different girls be cousins! Her parents would like her to be more like Aemilia, Calpurnia said, pulling a face. They would like us to be friends. I cannot think of an odder friend for Aemilia, or a better one for me. Mother has encouraged her to visit me again – so respectful and docile, she said, satisfied. She would not have said so if she had heard us at play this afternoon.

When I heard Aemilia's voice in the atrium, I felt like jumping into the clothes chest. I was certain that she had only come to pry. But after she had introduced Calpurnia, Aemilia seemed more interested in my gowns. "You wore such a pretty tunic at our party," she said. I looked at her cousin. Calpurnia looked as bored as me. "Let's dress up," I suggested.

"We could play Cleopatra," Calpurnia said, who had barely said a word up until then. She asked if the boys could join us – one to play Octavian, the other Antony.

"The boys won't want to do that," I exclaimed.

Nor did they – until they learned what Calpurnia had in mind. The battle of Actium!

"We can't play that!" Aemilia said, alarmed. "It is a nasty rough game."

"We're only pretending," Calpurnia protested. She took charge at once. "We need ships. This will be mine and Antony's," she said – sitting down on MY bed!

Marcus jumped on too. "I will be Antony," he said. He has taken quite a fancy to Calpurnia.

Aemilia said that such a game was beneath her dignity. Calpurnia and I caught each other's eyes. We were both trying not to laugh. But Aemilia was threatening to leave so I got out my knucklebones and we sat quietly tossing them. They did not stay long after that.

23 January

I have been wondering why I had never met Calpurnia before. Today I got my answer.

"But you have," she told me, crouching down next to me. She tossed a ball into the air. I was still breathless after our race. Calpurnia had won. No one is more fleet of foot than her. Marcus follows her round like a lovestruck puppy.

My face must have shown my puzzlement. "It was outside the Temple of Jupiter in the autumn," she said.

She laughed. "You looked as if you'd be sick when they sacrificed the bull."

"I did not!" I protested. Anyway, I told her, that was not a proper meeting.

"I remembered when we saw you in the street," Calpurnia said, and tossed the ball to me. "You looked as if you'd be sick then too."

The ball slipped through my fingers. If only she hadn't said that! As I fumbled for it, I tried to hide my hot face.

"I am glad we have met properly now," Calpurnia said. "Aemilia thinks of you as her best friend. I never thought a friend of hers could be a friend of mine."

28 January

I am so worried. It is over a week now since I last saw Aengus. In all that time I have not heard his owl-hoot once. Today I thought I had, but when I slipped out through the gate he wasn't there.

Why has he not come? Is he afraid to meet me now? What if Aemilia did see us together? But even if she did, would she tell her brother? My mind spins with it all. Oh, if only I knew what to think.

I'd saved Aengus a slice of pie. I didn't know what to do with it so I fed it to Pollux. I'd have eaten it myself, but I'd quite lost my appetite.

30 January

I have learned where Aengus is – languishing in one of the gladiators' cells. He has been sold to – I can scarcely bear to write this – to the gladiators' trainer.

I did not even have to pry it out of Aemilia. Marcus shouted the news as soon as he got home. Did he want all Pompeii to know? I am trying to hide how awful I feel, but at dinner I needed both hands to lift my glass to my mouth – they were trembling so much.

Marcus says that Aengus was sold for striking Ianuarius. I am sure that Aengus would never do anything so stupid. Why must Marcus believe everything that Gaius tells him? He says that Aengus is lucky to have found a new master at all. Lucky! To be sold to the gladiators' trainer? Humph! I don't think so. He said Quintus called him a bad lot. Always fighting. The arena is the proper place for such as him, he says. Of course the boys cannot wait to watch Aengus fight. He may as well be dead. He will never escape from Pompeii now. Never! Nor find his sister.

I do not believe that Aengus struck Ianuarius. Or – oh, think, Claudia, think – is that how he got his black eye? Did Ianuarius taunt him once too often? Is it the true reason he was sold? Somehow I must find out the truth. Oh bother. I see I have no choice but to speak to Aemilia. If he has been sold merely for speaking to *me*, I will never speak to *her* again.

Father has returned from Vastus's house, full of sympathy for Quintus. "Never buy a Briton," he said, shaking his head. "They are bad for business – always arguing and fighting." I put my head in my hands. Why must Father believe such lies?

Mother sighed. "Still, it is a terrible thing to be a gladiator," she said. I felt the tears trickle between my fingers. If only she hadn't said that.

"Why! Whatever is the matter, Claudia?" Mother asked. Her gentleness made me sob out loud. "That poor boy – he'll surely be killed," I cried.

"What a tender heart my little girl has," Father said, smiling. "Do not fret, child. Where there is life there is hope. The lad will not fight until he is trained. And – should he die – well, it is an honourable death. How many of us are so fortunate?"

"He's just a boy," I wailed. "He's too young to … to … d-die." I looked up through my wet fingers. Mother and Father were staring at me.

"We saw him at the slave auction," I said, hastily

swallowing down my tears. "Do you remember, Father? And he helped me home when I hurt my ankle. And … and … he worked for Quintus." I tried not to wince as I said the hated name. "I feel almost as if…" I searched vainly for the right words. What could I say? What would stop them looking at me like that? I lifted my head. "Almost as if he was one of our slaves."

Father took my hand in his and patted it. "Does it hurt very much that Quintus is betrothed to Iulia?" he asked, most tenderly. I flushed, but not for the reason Father thought. He squeezed my fingers. Oh, I felt guilty. Strictly speaking I had not told a lie, but I felt as if I had.

I forced a smile to my face, but my, it was hard.

FEBRUARIUS
3 February

I have just returned from Aemilia's house. She would not stop talking about Aengus. Almost I wanted to slap her. Now that Aengus is training to be a gladiator she is just as silly about him as she is about other boys. "Isn't he handsome," she sighed. "He'll fight from the chariot. Won't it be exciting to watch!"

Wild horses will not drag me to the arena. I will not watch

Aengus fight – on or off the chariot. And anyway, how did she know about that?

"Oh, aah, Father told me," said Aemilia vaguely. "He learned to drive the chariot at home in Britain."

"He should have been sold as a charioteer then," I said coldly.

And I still do not know the true reason why Aengus was sold. Aemilia said nothing at all about that, and I dared not pry too closely. Did Vastus always plan to sell Aengus to the lanista? He only bought him to outbid him. To show everyone how rich he was.

I thought that writing everything down would help. It hasn't. It has made me feel worse. Oh, why didn't I warn Aengus? Why didn't I say something?

I will not watch Aengus fight. Never. Never. Never. And I will stop up my ears when the games begin so I do not have to hear the crowds either.

4 February

I have put curses on Vastus and Quintus and buried them in the ground. I wrote the curses on a piece of metal I found in the street, so they will last for ever. "May misfortune overtake them," I whispered, patting the ground. I got up – and froze.

Someone was watching. Someone had followed me out of the side gate.

Marcus.

I trembled. Had he seen? Had he heard?

"What are you doing, Claudia?" he asked me.

"It's none of your business," I said. "Go away."

"I know what you're doing. You've put a curse on someone. I heard," he said stubbornly.

"So," I said defiantly. "So if I have."

He looked scared – as if he thought it was him I was cursing.

"Stupid," I said. "It's not you I've cursed."

He crept closer. "You need to sacrifice an animal," he said ghoulishly, "or it won't work."

"I can't do that," I said, shuddering. "It'll have to do as it is." I crouched down to pat the ground again. "Don't you ever come near this place again," I said fiercely, "or I'll … I'll…" I stopped, floundering. "You had better not," I said at last, lamely. But I don't think he will. He looked far too scared.

10 February

I have just returned from visiting Calpurnia's home, in the quarter of a thousand hammers as she calls it. I fancy I can still hear them ring. Calpurnia says you get used to it. And at least the smiths do not shout at night like the bakers. But then I am used to that.

Calpurnia took us to her father's workshop. (Her father is an armourer.) I knew I would not like it and I did not. I did not like any of it – the glow of the forge fire, the wicked-looking weapons shining blood-red in the firelight, the stacks of twisted metal and tools lying on the benches, the clanging and the hammering. I did not like the way the sparks flew off the anvil. It made me think of Vulcan in his mountain forge.

I almost cried out when we entered. A huge shadow was thrown across the wall – and for one awful moment I thought I was looking at Vulcan himself. Then I saw the big man sitting in the middle of the room, an apron over his tunic. In his left hand he held the tongs. In them was a piece of metal he was shaping with his hammer. It was his shadow I'd seen on the wall. Claudia, you are a silly!

It was a helmet for the gladiators, Calpurnia's father told us. Weren't the boys excited! They ran around the workshop gazing at the weapons, the shields and the helmets. I pulled Calpurnia aside.

"You never told me your father made the gladiators' armour," I hissed.

She smiled. "My father is a master craftsman." She showed me a helmet her father had already made. She touched it.

"Isn't it beautiful," she said, proudly. "The Murmillo will wear this. You will see it next in the arena."

No, Claudia will not!

We did not stop for long. A slave was pumping up the forge fire with a pair of bellows. He was shielded from the worst of the heat, but it was too hot in there for me. I wonder they can endure it. It must be awful in summer.

A wonderful thought has just struck me. As Calpurnia's father makes the gladiators' armour, he must visit the gladiators' barracks. Maybe I will be able to glean news of Aengus. Oh, how pleased I am. Pleased, pleased, pleased! But I must ask my questions carefully, or Calpurnia will become suspicious.

19 February

Have little time to write. Uncle is staying for the festival. What a strain Uncle's visits always are.

All the temples are closed. It is a solemn time – this time when we honour our dead. A sad time too for Mother and Father. There is nowhere they can go to mourn their dead. All we can hope is that they are at peace.

Yesterday we walked across the city to the Nucerian Gate, bearing food, wine and flowers. Uncle brought the wine from his farm. And that is fair, as it was his wife and dead children we had come to honour. Their tombs lie outside the city, in the City of the Dead.

Even when it is full of families like now, that place makes my skin crawl. What lurks behind the tall still cypress trees and the silent tombs? What strange instinct made Pollux run here of all places? To this city where only the dead dwell?

As Father poured the wine and scattered a little salt for the Manes, the gods of the dead, I crept up to Mother. She had her arms around the boys, holding them close. She reached out to draw me near too – as if afraid that lost souls would seize me and bear me away to that dark world under our feet. I clung tightly to her.

Somewhere, far off, trumpets sounded faintly. We jumped and looked uneasily round at each other. Who was blowing those trumpets – someone alive or dead? "Some poor person is being taken to their last resting place," Mother said softly.

"Aye," Uncle muttered. "Let us hope that it is not a child, gone ahead of its parents." Mother says Uncle had five children, and all of them are dead now.

There are other cemeteries too; one beyond the Salt Gate at the west of the city. Father says it is named after the salt pans where seawater is evaporated to make salt. To reach them you walk under great arched gates. The tombs line the road, which carries on down to Herculaneum and Neapolis. I think you have to be very rich to be buried there. Some of those tombs are very grand indeed. Gaius told Sextus that his family tomb is there. It would be!

21 February

I am cross. Father has persuaded Uncle to stay on a while, and it is our special family day tomorrow. Father and my brothers will be home all day. Uncle will quite spoil it. Grumble. Grumble. Grumble. Nothing in the town is good. Everything about the countryside is better. I wonder he visits us at all.

I crept round to the bakery to seek comfort from Pollux. I hauled him on to my lap, and he gave my nose a sad lick. He did not look very pleased to see me. "What – just you!" his eyes seemed to say. Does he understand that Aengus will not come back? And suddenly – looking into Pollux's mournful face – I felt so unutterably sad. I buried my face in his coat and wept.

24 February

Uncle returned to his farm today. Rarely have I seen him as merry as he was last night. He plied Father with wine. "And a glass for the little lass." Watered down, of course.

"Be careful not to spill it," he said to me. Will he never let me forget my clumsy fingers? Mind, Mother showed him the blanket I wove. Uncle looked quite surprised. A housewifely task the little lass can do well. My, my… "Has a husband been found for her," I heard him ask Father. I pray not.

MARTIUS
1 March

It is the day we honour our mothers. I have done my best to be good but it is not easy to be dutiful and obedient all the time. How do other girls manage it? I made Mother a gift, too – a skein of spun thread. I am very proud of it. I spun it all myself – and, for once, there is not a single knot in it. Mother gave me a big hug. "You could not have given me anything I would like more," she said. "You are a good girl, Claudia. And one day you will make someone a good wife." Ugh!

5 March

Calpurnia suspects I am hiding something from her, and it annoys her. "I think of you as a sister," she told me – even though she has not known me long. "Sisters tell each other everything," she said, doodling with her bare toe on the floor. "Don't you trust me?"

I told her I did, but I felt my face flush.

Calpurnia talks a lot about the games. She goes to watch the gladiators fight – as often as she can, she says.

"Ugh," I said, shuddering. "How can you enjoy that?" Straightaway I realized it had been the wrong thing to say.

She gave me a searching look. "Why then do you ask so many questions about the gladiators?" she said.

"My brothers want to know," I gabbled quickly – hating myself for lying.

I must be more careful. Anyway I have found out nothing useful – beyond that there is a new recruit. As if I didn't know who *that* was. A tiro, Calpurnia calls him. I asked if she had seen him, and was he a good fighter. But she could not even tell me if he was British!

Calpurnia is still trying to persuade me to go to the games. I'd sooner marry Quintus, I told her. You should thank the gods you are not, she said. He is both spoilt and cruel. At one time she thought she would be matched to him. But, she said, she told her father she'd sooner throw herself under a wagon or be torn apart by wild beasts than marry a fellow like that. I don't believe her. Like me Calpurnia will have to do as her father wishes.

15 March

Each year we celebrate the festival of Anna Parenna on Uncle's farm. I wish we could picnic by the River Sarno like other Pompeiians. But Father will not allow it. Only the truly vulgar do that, he says.

It was late when we set off. As we were about to leave, a message came for Father – his old master's son wished to see him. So off he had to go. By the time we reached the Vesuvius Gate, all the carts had been taken – except for one. And no wonder that no one had hired this one. A rickety old thing it was – one wheel wobbling on its axle – and the nag, a poor old thing. It shuffled a few steps, and stopped. Marcus hit it with a stick, but it turned its head and gave him such a sad look. So I hopped off and tried to coax it forward with the apple I'd saved for the journey. It thanked me by dribbling all over my hand. Ugh!

We passed by fields that had just been ploughed. Slaves were bent over them, hoeing and digging, planting vegetables, and scattering seed. As I looked at them, I found myself wondering what the Britons grow on their farms. Everything around me was as fresh and green as my apple. In Britain, Aengus has told me, the fields stay green even in summer. They do not grow brown and dusty like ours.

Uncle came off the fields to greet us. It is a busy time of year for farmers. "You are growing soft, brother," he said, giving Father's arm a playful punch. "What has happened to those fine muscles!" Father was a champion wrestler in his youth.

Father and Uncle are so funny! Father says that Anna Parenna fed the Roman army with bread baked by her own hand. We bakers should honour her, he says. But Uncle says nonsense, the festival is named after a river. And they argue about it. Every year they have the same argument.

After a time Sextus disappeared to gather those shiny stones he likes to collect and Marcus to ride Uncle's horse. I trailed after him. Marcus fancies himself as a charioteer but he could not even mount the horse. I jeered as he jumped and grabbed at its back, his hands sliding down the sleek coat again and again. What a lot of fuss he made! Then he found a stone to climb up by, and I gave him a shove too. Up he went again, grabbing at the horse's mane. That was a bad mistake. The horse turned its head and nosed him off. Back Marcus toppled – right into the dung pit.

He was a sight! I helped him clean himself, pulling up handfuls of grass to rub off the muck. But that just made it worse. Not that anyone minded. Not as they had when I spilt my grape juice. It is not fair. Uncle just said he was a true country boy. He certainly smelt like one. Mother would not let him ride home in the cart with us. Ha! I sat at the back, holding my nose as he trailed slowly behind. It is a fair walk back to the town, so I did feel a bit sorry for him. Mind, it might have been quicker if we had all walked – more comfortable too. That horse must have walked through every pothole and over every stone.

Sextus is funny about his stones. He ran away to hide them when we got back. No one knows where he keeps them. Mother says it shows that he'll be a careful man when he grows up, Father that he'll be a miser. I hide my precious things away. And I have secrets too. What does that say about me?

I nearly forgot! As we pulled up at the Vesuvius Gate I saw Ancient sitting in his usual place, hand outstretched. He looked so tired and hungry that I ran up and gave him some of my olives.

"Why, it's the child," he said. His eyes roamed about,

before coming to rest on me. "You do not have your dog today? Where is he?"

"At home, Ancient, guarding the bakery."

"Have you attended to what I told you?" he asked. I nodded nervously.

He smiled. "Let your dog be your guide. He understands." He tapped his nose.

I backed away. What did Pollux understand? Why must Ancient talk in riddles?

I do feel sorry for Ancient though – all alone, and no one to care for him. Grandfather died a beggar. Mother says that anyone who sold his own son into slavery deserved to end his life as he did. But Father says that Grandfather simply could not afford to care for all his children, and at least none of them were put out to die.

23 March

The boys returned to school today. How quiet the house is without them. Sextus did not want to go. He finds it hard to learn his letters and Marcus says the teacher often hits him for his slowness. Father thinks they are lucky to go to school at all. Life is full of hardship, he says. This is a lesson everyone needs to learn – as much as to read and write. I feel sorry for the boys, school is a harsh place, but Father is right. And poor Father learned more about hardship than anything else when he was a boy. He did not go to school. He was a slave – and had to pick up any learning as best he could.

25 March

As Mother and I walked down the Street of Abundance this morning some words on a wall caught my eye. They were written in big bold letters by a proper sign-writer so they were easy to read, unlike many of the scribblings on Pompeii's walls. Some of what is written is so rude it makes me blush. This was a notice about the games soon to be held in Pompeii.

I read it aloud to Mother, trying to keep the wobble out of my voice. There will be fights from the chariot, it said. I tell myself that Aengus will not fight – that he has barely begun his training. But is that not why the lanista bought him? What did Aemilia say to me? "He will fight from the chariot." Oh Isis, please do not let Aengus fight. Please keep him safe. *Please*. I will be good. I will do whatever Mother and Father ask of me.

27 March

The boys talk of nothing but the games now. I think Marcus has been running round Pompeii reading all the notices. I am sick of it. There will be a fight between a Thracian and a Murmillo, he said. The Retiarius will fight too. Sextus likes the Retiarius. "How do you know?" I demanded. Sextus has never seen any gladiator fight. He told me there is a picture of a Retiarius drawn on the house across the street. He has a trident and a net, in which he tries to hook his prey. Ugh!

Later I saw the drawing for myself. Next to it some wag has scribbled that he is the girls' heart-throb. Humph!

The names of the gladiators who will fight are written on the walls. Aengus's isn't amongst them, but then some of the names are very odd – like Hermes, the messenger god, or Tigris, the tiger. Calpurnia says they aren't the gladiators' real names, they are the names they are known by when they fight. So I'm none the wiser.

APRILIS
3 April

Samius and Chius have gone to watch the gladiators at their banquet. It is a sort of last feast for them, the evening before they fight. Anyone who wishes can watch. Yesterday the gladiators were paraded before the public in the Forum. It is horrible that. The boys begged to go but Mother would not let them.

4 April

I was sitting with Mother today when a huge roar reached us – carried all the way from the arena. I put my hands over my ears. I cannot bear to hear it. Father says the games are good for business. Mother thinks they bring ruffians into the town.

I think Mother is right. When I went round to the bakery earlier, two youths were fighting on the street corner. They were pretending to be gladiators, but I'd not have bet on either. The queue outside the bakery cheered them on. Then a woman in a flat overhead stuck out her head and bawled at them to stop. They had woken her baby and it was crying, she said. The lads stopped just long enough to laugh. They were to be sorry for their rudeness. A moment later a bucket of slops was emptied over their heads. Disgusting! But it ended the fight fast enough. I watched them go. One was limping, the other had a black eye. And they stank! Stupid.

Outside, the boys have their wooden swords out. Clatter, clatter, clatter. Fight, fight, fight! Is it all they care about? Father is proud of them. Manly, he says they are!

8 April

Mother won't let Sextus go to the arena. So Father has bought him a toy trident. It has a picture of a Retiarius stamped on its side. Ugh!

This afternoon I saw the wild beasts taken to the arena. I clutched Fausta's arm while their cages clattered past – they looked none too safe. Inside the first cage sat a tiger. His dark eyes looked sadly at me.

Behind him rattled a pair of wolves. Their noses were pressed close to the bars. Poor things! I wished I could open their cages and let them out.

12 April

I feel sick. Aengus will fight, Marcus says. It will be on the day before the Ides of May.

I wheedled out of him how he knew. Gaius told him, he said. "Why must you believe everything Gaius says?" I said crossly, but I felt my hands tremble in my lap. It must be true, if he even knows the date.

13 April

My secret is out! Last night, as I prepared for bed, I burst into tears. Fausta tried to comfort me. "How can I help you, child, if you will not tell me what upsets you," she said. And so, heart thumping, I did. I *had* to tell someone. Writing down how you feel does not always help. But I feel worse now. I have broken my promise to Aengus. Fausta wiped my eyes.

"He will never fight in the arena, child," she said. I looked deep into her clouded eye. Her words do not comfort me at all. How can Fausta be so sure about something like this?

MAIUS
14 May

I went to the arena today. I – who said I never would! But I have made myself a solemn promise now. I will never ever go to the arena again, no matter who is fighting. We arrived in the early afternoon. The wild beast fights had finished – as Calpurnia had promised – but such shouts and screams met us as we clambered up the staircase to our place at the top of the arena.

We had arrived too early. In the arena criminals were still being slaughtered. I looked down and away hastily. But the horror of what I saw in that brief moment is still imprinted on my mind. In one corner a man was being dragged away by a hook, while someone scattered fresh sand over the bloodstained ground. Two more men, their necks roped together, were trying to run from a great tiger. It leaped forward. One of the men tripped, pulling the other prisoner down with him. I pressed my hands to my ears to shut out the screams, until I heard Calpurnia whisper that it was over.

I was furious. How could they have brought me to such a spectacle. Calpurnia's face was white. "I did not know," she whispered. "I promise."

I told her I didn't care a fig for her promises, and turned to go. And then I saw Aemilia squashed up on the far side of Calpurnia's mother. "I did not expect to see you here, Claudia," she said, sounding surprised. I tossed my head proudly. I would stay. I would not let Aemilia see that I cared.

The harsh notes of trumpets blared and we craned forward – the great gates had been thrown open. My heart was pounding as my eyes scanned the arena. Would Aengus be amongst the troupe of men marching in?

I leaned forward as far as I could. Far below I could make out a platform borne high, on which I was told were statues of the god Mars and the hero Hercules, and the palm branch that would later honour the brows of the victors.

Last of all, the gladiators. I stared at the men marching around the arena, the sun blazing on their helmets. The gladiators' supporters were shouting themselves hoarse. I dug my fingers into my palms until they hurt. Was Aengus amongst those men? Would he fight today? Or had Fausta been right?

The procession marched out and the games began. Over the eager chattering Calpurnia tried to explain what would happen now. First, the prelude. "The gladiators fight, but only with their blunted training weapons," she said. "Then they will be paired. That's when the real fighting begins." I nodded, but I was barely listening. My eye was still searching for Aengus among all the people in the arena. There were the musicians, and over by the wall, the assistants, holding the gladiators' weapons and helmets. And who was that man in a long tunic with a long stick? "The referee," Calpurnia said. "He uses his stick to mark the sand and on any gladiator who refuses to fight." I winced. Why must she say such awful things? She touched my arm. "Now they are checking the gladiators' weapons. See, Claudia?" I looked away quickly, my mind imagining the harsh scrape of iron on iron. How fervently I wished that I had not come.

A huge cheer went up. Unable to stop myself, I looked down. Two chariots had driven into the arena in a whirlwind of dust and sand. I clenched my hands into fists. My heart was beating so fast that I felt quite sick, but I could not look away now. I craned forwards again. If only I could see their faces... If only... The awnings flapped like sails over our heads. Far below someone was crouching over by the wall – a boy with reddish hair. Aengus! Calpurnia nudged me. "That's the tiro," she said. Relief made me dizzy. Aengus would not fight.

I remembered what Aengus had told me about chariot-fighting. But this – this was different. It was a fight to the death, between two men, to entertain us, the spectators. Round the arena the chariots raced, the crowd bawling, trumpets blaring. Even I was cheering! And then – just as the men were preparing to jump down and fight – one of the horses reared. Something had frightened it. The charioteer fell back, tumbling out of the chariot, the ends of the reins twisted round his waist. Released of its driver, the horse galloped forward, the chariot swinging wildly behind it. The crowd gasped as the hapless charioteer was dragged along the ground. I covered my face with my hands. Calpurnia pinched my arm. I shook her off. "Look!" she cried. "Look!"

"I cannot," I hissed, listening to the chariots rumble, the crowd shouting. Suddenly the crowd fell silent. Was it over? Was the charioteer dead? Next to me I heard Calpurnia gasp. I opened my eyes.

Aengus had sprinted forward. How fast he ran! Then – just as the horse and its empty chariot were almost upon him – he leaped for the terrified horse's head, pulling at the harness. Nimbly he swung himself up onto the horse's back, laying his head close against its mane, pulling the horse round, out of the way of the other chariot, which was racing fast towards him. Would they crash? Would they? I could feel the blood pounding in my ears. The chariot skidded past, missing Aengus by a hair's breadth. I let out my breath with a long sigh. Aengus was still holding on to his horse. It shuddered, coming to a halt at last. Men bearing a stretcher raced into the arena to tend to the injured gladiator, still caught in the reins. Then – to the cheers of the crowd – Aengus drove the chariot round and out of the arena.

They had not had a fight, but the crowd went wild. Everyone was as one, on their feet, waving their togas, cheering the young Briton.

106

"Who is he?" I heard someone ask behind me. "He looks like a prince." My heart felt as if it was bursting inside me. I was so proud.

I should have left then. Instead I settled myself down to watch, chattering excitedly to Calpurnia. The referee drew a line in the sand with his long stick. Calpurnia pointed out the two gladiators preparing to fight. One was dressed in a loincloth, a plumed helmet on his head. Like his opponent, a visor covered his face. In one hand he grasped a painted shield, which reached nearly to his shoulder. In the other, he held a straight broad sword.

"The Murmillo," Calpurnia said, pointing.

"How do you know?" I asked her, interested in spite of myself.

"Remember the helmet I showed you? It is brimmed, with a horsehair crest. Sometimes the Murmillo fights the Hoplomachus but today he faces the Thracian."

"And how do you know that?" I asked wonderingly.

"The Thracian wears a griffin-crested helmet. Look, Claudia." I stared at the man, far below us in the arena. He carried a squarish shield, his short, curved sword held behind it.

The Murmillo stood, left shoulder and left foot forward, and raised his shield. Suddenly the Thracian pounced, but the other caught him with the edge of his shield. The Thracian stumbled back, his foot skidding in the sand. In the crowd, his supporters groaned. But he righted himself fast, poised again to thrust, searching for exposed flesh. He leaped again, but his sword went wide. Then back and forwards, thrusting, parrying and thrusting again, the sand scuffing up in a cloud so it was hard to see anything clearly. Now they were both on the ground. The Murmillo had his sword raised high over the other's squirming body. The Thracian lowered his sword arm, and raised his hand.

"An appeal for mercy," Calpurnia whispered to me. "It is over now. It is up to us whether the Thracian lives or dies." Did she *have* to say that? The referee ran up and pinioned the Murmillo's sword arm behind his back, so that he could not injure the Thracian further. Then he looked up at us. What was the crowd's will? Should the Thracian live or die? Would the Murmillo be ordered to deliver the death-blow on his comrade? The man dressed as Charon stood by, his club grasped in his hand, eyes on the man squirming on the ground. Would he have to use it? Would the vanquished Thracian be dispatched to the Underworld? Up until then I'd actually been enjoying myself. But with a shock I recalled what this was truly about – a man's life and death – and just to entertain us. I looked away, shuddering. I was disgusted at myself.

"Iugula. Iugula," a lone voice called suddenly – no doubt one of the Murmillo's supporters. "Kill him. Kill him."

I glanced at Calpurnia's face – it was as pale as I was sure mine must be. Aemilia looked as if she was about to be sick.

I found myself leaning forward. "Mitte!" I cried. "Spare

him!" How thin my voice sounded, echoing around the great bowl of the arena. "Mitte!" I cried again, as loudly as I could. Why did no one join me? Did they want him dead? He'd fought well and bravely. Spare him!

"Mitte!" Calpurnia and Aemilia's voices joined mine. "Mitte! Mitte!" The cry was taken up and I saw people lift the hems of their tunics and wave their togas. I let out my breath with a deep sigh. The Thracian would be spared.

But I'd had enough. I didn't care if the fighting was skilful or not. It was bloody and horrible. What choice do those poor men have? One gladiator did not want to fight. An assistant prodded him with a red-hot iron until he did. I remembered an animal fight I'd seen once – how the poor creature had to be goaded till it fought – and how I'd sworn then I'd never watch a fight again. What was I doing at this terrible place?

At the end we stumbled down the stairs. I felt hot, sick and thirsty. The crowds jostled past us, hoping for glimpses of the gladiators. Calpurnia and Aemilia were chattering excitedly about the "young British chieftain'". I felt like thumping them. What nonsense they were talking. He was just a boy. A mere barbarian boy who'd showed all those Romans what skill and courage truly was. "A lad as skilled as that will surely be put to the test soon," I heard a man say. I glowered at him. Had he not been tested already? Was that not enough for them? Father asked how I'd enjoyed myself. I told him that I never wanted to see another gladiator fight as long as I lived.

It was horrible! He laughed and laughed. I can't think why. I don't think it's funny at all.

21 May

Calpurnia has discovered my secret. We were talking about the games – me changing the subject as usual – when suddenly I realized that she wasn't listening to me. I might as well have been chattering to myself. I stopped, uneasy. "Everyone is talking about that tiro," she said quietly. "Everyone – except you. Why?" She gave me a long look and I gulped. I had not realized my silence would make her suspicious of me. But I could not – would not – break my word to Aengus. Calpurnia looked disappointed. "I thought we were friends," she said sadly. "You are not my friend if you cannot trust me."

"I do…" I began, but stopped, blushing. What could I say?

"You do not trust me," she said, stubbornly.

"That is not true!" I cried.

"Then prove it to me," she said.

"I made a promise," I told her. "I would tell you if I could."

She nodded. "I understand. You must not break your word." She paused and looked up at me – and I saw in her face what I'd always wondered. She knew. She had seen us in the street – Aengus and me. And just as I was thinking that she said: "I did see him and you together. You and that tiro."

"You said nothing to me," I said.

Calpurnia nodded. "I hoped you would tell me." We were silent for a time.

"How did you know who he was?" I asked at last.

"I'd seen him in Quintus's bakery."

"Did Aemilia recognize him?"

"She must have – if I did. Oh, Claudia, how many boys in Pompeii have hair that red, skin that fair?"

I looked up at her. She must have, she had said. "Don't you know for sure?"

Calpurnia looked cross. "If you mean, did Aemilia say anything to me? No, she didn't. Aemilia may be silly, but she is loyal. She would not betray your secret – any more than I would."

I swallowed. I remembered how Aemilia had visited me when I had twisted my ankle, how she'd even wished me to marry her brother. She had been loyal and I – I felt ashamed.

But – oh, Isis! – I had broken my word to Aengus – again. Calpurnia seemed to read my mind. "You have not betrayed him. I already knew," she said.

It was true. I had not broken my word. But… I felt my cheeks grow hot. What would Calpurnia think? Me – a freeborn Roman girl – befriending a barbarian slave boy!

"He is brave," she said suddenly. "I wish I could meet him."

I felt a huge rush of relief. "I am glad you know," I said

suddenly. "I'd so wanted to tell you." I told her what Marcus had said. "I am afraid that he will be made to fight soon."

"No, he won't," Calpurnia said. "He won't fight until he is trained. The lanista won't allow a promising tiro to fight before he is ready."

"Our slave Fausta told me that he would never fight in the arena," I said slowly.

Calpurnia looked puzzled. "How could she know something like that?"

"I don't know," I said. "Sometimes Fausta says the strangest things. I am sure she sees things that others don't. And then Ancient…"

"Ancient?"

"An old beggar, who sits at the Vesuvius Gate. Oh Calpurnia, he said such things – such awful, frightening things." And then it all poured out – the things I've been trying so hard to forget. Oh, the relief to talk about it. I told her everything – about the day the ground shook, all the portents I'd noted and what Ancient had said.

"But, Claudia, the ground often shakes in Pompeii," Calpurnia pointed out – just as Father had. "Anyway that was months ago."

"Even so, it must mean something," I said stubbornly. Then I told her about my dream.

Calpurnia looked scared. "Have you told anyone else about it?"

"Only Fausta," I said.

"What did she say?" Calpurnia asked curiously.

"That our fate lies in the hands of the gods," I said.

Calpurnia snorted. "That is no answer. Why did you not tell your parents? They could have consulted the augurs. They would have explained your dream."

"I was afraid to. And – I've been trying to forget."

"But you haven't," Calpurnia pointed out. She rested her chin on her hands, looking thoughtful. "I know," she said eagerly. "We will write down everything we notice – every strange sight or sound. Then we will consult the augurs."

I've promised her I will, but now I wish I hadn't. I don't want to know what it all means. Not now. It frightens me. I want to forget.

31 May

Calpurnia is a true friend. She spent the whole of yesterday afternoon with Aemilia, hoping to hear news of Aengus.

"All we did was try out new hairstyles and make-up," she grumbled. "I heard nothing useful at all." She has found out nothing from her father either.

We wish there was a way to help Aengus escape, but

Calpurnia says he will be kept locked up when he is not training. I told Calpurnia about his sister. "If only we knew where she was," I said sadly. I used to be pleased that Aengus hadn't found her, as I was afraid they'd run away together. Now I wish he had. In the bakery he'd had a chance of escape. He had none now. I described her to Calpurnia. Calpurnia looked startled. "I have seen a girl who looks like that."

"Where?" I asked eagerly.

"In Stephanus's laundry."

I shook my head. "Yes, she was there, but she was turned away long ago when they found out that she was left-handed."

"Poor girl," said Calpurnia softly. "I don't think we will find her now." Then she asked me if I had seen anything interesting. Any portents. I was pleased to say I hadn't. "Neither have I," she said. She sounded almost as if she was sorry!

IUNIUS
22 June

I am ashamed. I have not kept up my diary. But then I have less need of it – now that I have Calpurnia to confide in. Anyway papyrus is precious. I must not waste it.

I still have not seen anything curious – but Calpurnia

has. Yesterday, she told me, a boy caught fire, but was not burned. Without doubt, that is an omen. Her father consulted the augurs.

"What did he learn?" I asked nervously.

"A lode was missing from the liver," she said with relish.

"What does that mean?" I asked, shuddering.

Calpurnia shrugged. *I* think he was probably a charlatan. Father says there are augurs aplenty wandering the streets these days, and that many of them are charlatans and we must be careful who we listen to.

I saw an augur in the street today. I knew he was an augur by the conical hat he wore and the curved staff he was leaning on. He was there when we went to the Forum and he was still there when we got back. His eyes scanned the sky, so I looked up too. I could not look for long, the glare hurt my eyes. I couldn't see anything – not even a bird flew past. But there must have been something very interesting for he was doing good business amongst our customers.

30 June

The grain ships have arrived from Alexandria. Sextus begged to go to the port to see them. Stupid! Puteoli port is too far away. But Father had business with a grain merchant at Pompeii docks so he took us there instead. Mother stayed at home. She is always sad when the grain ships arrive. They bring news and mail from Mother's homeland as well as grain – but there is never any news for Mother.

We stood amongst the crowds, watching as the barges were towed up the river, flies clinging like a dark cloud to the slaves' sweaty backs. One barge was already in harbour, settled comfortably into the water like a fat Roman matron. A man shouted orders, a plank was thrown down and goods were passed ashore. A scribe stood nearby – checking the cargo, Sextus told us. Sextus was our eyes. Perched on Father's shoulders he could see far more than the rest of us. One slave dropped his sack on the ground. It burst right open, the grain spilling out like sand. People dived upon it, scooping up the grain in their tunics. I heard the slave cry out as he was pushed roughly aside.

After Father had finished his business we pushed our way back through the docks, past the big warehouses, crowded with dealers and merchants, past the factory where they make fish sauce – my, how that stinks! – and up through the press of people and wagons to the city gates. The laughter of soldiers at the watchtower, the hammering of builders working on a new house in the city walls, drifted down to us. I felt happy, safe and comfortable.

And it was then, just as I was walking through the gate,

that I thought I felt something – a ripple, a faint shuddering of the ground under my feet. It was so slight, I wonder now if I imagined it. I pray so. I have written it down all the same.

IULIUS
5 July

I am upset. I have quarrelled with Calpurnia. All over a stupid omen.

We had been talking about the Apollo Games. The acrobatics were marvellous, Calpurnia said. One man balanced on one hand alone, while blowing fire out of his mouth.

I was most envious. If I had not fainted at the bull-goading I'd have seen the acrobatics for myself. I had not even wanted to see the poor bull goaded. But Marcus had pulled us over to watch, and Father had said that we must stay together.

"It is an omen," Calpurnia said with much certainty.

"What is?" I asked.

"The man breathing fire," she said impatiently. "You are not listening, Claudia."

"More likely a trick," I said grumpily. I was still feeling sore that I'd missed it. Then I said I wanted to stop writing down omens anyway.

"What have you written?" she asked me quickly. "You told me you hadn't noticed anything."

"I haven't—" I began. And stopped. Hadn't the ground shaken again a few days ago? I wasn't sure, but I just knew I didn't want to talk about it.

"Tell me," she wheedled.

Then I lost my temper. "To you it's just a game," I snapped. "But it's much more than a game to me."

Calpurnia looked startled. "How can you say that?"

"Because it's true," I muttered. And I got up and left.

10 July

I have not seen Calpurnia since we quarrelled. Good! I do not want to see her. I do not want to play her stupid games.

11 July

I saw Calpurnia in the street this afternoon. She was on her way to see me, I to see her. We are friends again.

I am glad. But – I have told her again – I will not write down any more portents.

25 July

I pick up my pen though I am weary of writing. I have been busy these past days helping Father with his letters. And when I have finished them I do not feel like writing anything else. But I must put down the big things and today I learned something most important.

EMPEROR VESPASIAN HAS DIED

Father says it is sad news, and I am sad, but I am excited too. Something has just struck me. Could the emperor's death be the true reason for all those portents? Could that even be why the ground shook last year? And why it trembled again last month? What could be more important or momentous than the death of our emperor?

AUGUSTUS
10 August

Awful news! Calpurnia is leaving Pompeii! Her father is going into business with her uncle in Rome. "I came as soon as Father told me," she said breathlessly, throwing herself down next to me. She says she does not want to leave, but she seems very excited. "They are building a great arena for the games in the city," she told me. "It will be colossal – the biggest amphitheatre in the empire," she added proudly.

"When are you leaving?" I asked her, hoping it would not be soon.

"In September," Calpurnia said.

"That is not long," I said sadly.

"It is in a month," Calpurnia said. "We will see each other often before I go."

I nodded. I was close to tears. I'd lost one friend, and now I was about to lose another.

"You will always be my friend, Claudia," Calpurnia said. "Promise you will visit me."

As if I wouldn't promise that.

"Come to the games when the amphitheatre opens," she

said, and then she saw my face and laughed. "No, I will not ask you to them."

Somehow I managed a smile. "No, I will never watch another gladiator fight," I told her.

I'll miss her so much.

23 August

I have nearly finished the second scroll, so I am writing in the tiniest letters I can. Today is the Feast of Vulcan, so this evening Father took us to the Forum to make our sacrifice to the god. I threw a wriggling fish into the fire and stepped back fast, hating to see how it writhed and sizzled. And then I thought about what Ancient had said. Vulcan is angry he'd told me. And I felt relieved then that I'd made my sacrifice. If Vulcan is still angry our sacrifice will appease him – won't it? It was a hot evening, but I felt myself shiver as I stared up at Vesuvius.

SEPTEMBRIS
10 September

I end the second scroll with the saddest of news. Calpurnia left Pompeii today.

SCROLL THE THIRD
OCTOBRIS
12 October

I have not written my diary since Calpurnia left. I felt too sad to write and anyway I had nothing to write on. Then this morning I found this scroll. It was lying on the chest at the end of my bed. No one can tell me how it got there, but when I saw it I felt as if I'd had a sign – a sign that I should begin my diary again. And I am glad of it now; for I am sure that something is amiss.

The animals are upset. Whenever Pollux sees me he whimpers, and yesterday evening, when I went to take him for a walk, he refused to leave the bakery. I coaxed him on to my lap. His whole body was shuddering, as if something had badly frightened him. Then this morning I saw that his ears were cocked, as if he was listening for something. The donkeys are restless too. Chius says they walk round and round, snorting and braying. I know – they woke even me last night.

"Will we consult the augurs?" I said to Father, but he just said, "Oh, Claudia, don't be foolish, nothing has upset the animals. You are surely not worrying about that crack." Well, I am. I have seen that crack – it is a new one, and I am sure that it has got bigger, though I do not know how. I grumbled to Marcus but Marcus says that Father has his mind on other matters. There is to be a banquet at Vastus's house, he said – as if it was something really important.

Bother Vastus. Bother the stupid banquet.

What did Aengus tell me? The animals hear things that we can not. But what do they hear? What are they trying to tell me? If only Aengus were here, he would help me. Inside, my stomach feels all knotted. It is because – like the animals – I just *know* that something is wrong – even if I don't know quite what. Mother thinks that I am sickening for something, and that it is hardly surprising if I do not eat properly. I ate more at lunch to please her. But I do not feel any better.

20 October

I can barely keep my pen steady. The ground has begun to shake again!

I do not need to stick my finger into the cracks to see that they have grown bigger now. The house still stands, Father says firmly. As does Pompeii. There is no need to fret about the tremors. We will find a plasterer to repair the cracks. I wish I felt reassured – but I don't.

It began at breakfast this morning. At first we didn't know what was happening. Our beakers and plates began to rattle and then they slid down the table, as if they had a life of their own. It was most peculiar, as well as frightening. I managed to grab my beaker before it fell off the table. Sextus was not so lucky. His tumbled into his lap. He was soaked.

When I stepped outside later I nearly tripped over a workman. He was scratching his head, gazing at something in the pavement. I stared down too. And what did I see? A crack – a deep one – running right down it. I followed it to see how far it went – all the way to the water tower at the crossroads.

The water supply to the Stabian Baths has failed. No one seems to know why. As we made our way there today we saw people protesting on the Forum steps. An official came across to speak to them, his white toga flapping importantly. They swarmed round him like angry hornets, waving their fists and shouting. There is much talk about the tremors. Some are afraid worse is to come and mutter about leaving. They are portents of disaster, they say. There will be another great earthquake. Just wait and see. Others scoff, echoing Father's words: tremors are common in Pompeii. But on the way back from the baths I saw a wagon trundle down the street, children squashed in between the chests and blankets. One family at least has taken heed of the warnings. If only Father would. I jumped when I heard the wheels of that wagon rumble past. It may sound silly but that is how you know the ground is about to shake. First it makes that rumbling noise and then it trembles. Each time I hear that sound now I jump, thinking that there will be another tremor.

21 October

Awoke this morning to find my nostrils full of smoke. I pulled my cloak over my nose and mouth and ran coughing into the atrium. Smoke billowed round it and curled upwards – grey against the blue, like clouds. A fire had broken out in the kitchen. Our well is nearly dry, so Father ordered Felix, one of the household slaves, to run to the bakery for sand.

If Fausta had not woken early we might all have been burned in our beds! The walls and roof of the kitchen are black with smoke. As are all the pots, the ladles, the jars – everything. The household slaves spent most of the morning scrubbing them with handfuls of damp sand. How the kitchen caught fire, no one knows. "For sure it is a bad omen," I heard Xenia say to Fortunata. I wish the slaves would not gossip amongst themselves.

Father is cheerful though. He has found a plasterer to fill the cracks. And that is some feat, as plasterers are in much demand now. Many houses have cracks that need repairing.

He started with the bakery. The counter has cracked and there is a bad split on the wall by the oven. The scaffolding is up now, and the plasterer whistles as he slaps on the fresh plaster – as if he has not a care in the world.

Sextus has lost his pet mouse. He is most upset. Marcus says that it has run away, that all the mice have gone, and it's true, I haven't seen or heard them either – not even scratching across the floor at night. Mice leave a house when it's about to collapse, I am told. But our house will not collapse – will it? Oh, Claudia, why did you write that?

22 October

I saw Ancient this morning. He has left the Vesuvius Gate, and says he will not return there. Such strange things he has seen on Vesuvius. Vapours rising from the earth. Springs that have dried up. "Some say that the long-buried giants are stirring again. Indeed, that they have been seen on the mountain," he said. "I – I say simply that the mountain is stirring." I felt my mouth grow dry, and I licked my lips nervously. I did not like this talk of mountains and giants stirring.

"Then why do you stay in Pompeii?" I asked him, and felt foolish as soon as the words were out of my mouth. How could a poor lame old beggar walk all the way to safety in another town?

Ancient merely smiled. "I will leave soon. The gods will tell me when and where to go."

I told Father what he said, but Father says I should not believe everything I hear. "The tremors are caused by air trapped underground, just as thunderclaps are caused by air trapped in clouds," he told me patiently. All sorts of stories are flying round the town, he says. Many are plainly untrue. Father is more worried about the water. It has been dry for so long, but even when it rains our well never seems to get any fuller. Aemilia told me today that their water is down to a trickle. Water to private houses is always turned off first when there is a shortage. Vastus has been to the government offices to find out when it will be restored, but no one can tell him when that will be. There is water aplenty at the public fountains he was told. Her father is so angry, she said. The pipes that should bring water into the house hiss and bang – only a dirty trickle dribbles out. It has a funny smell too. I told her it could not be as bad as the smell from our latrine. I have to hold my nose tight when I visit it. Flies swarm round me when I enter. Ugh!

But I am far more worried about Aengus. I hate to think of him locked up in the barracks. What if the tremors get worse? How will he get out? I try and push these thoughts away, but they keep coming back to trouble me, and there is nothing I can do about it. Nothing I can do to help him. I hate feeling so helpless.

Poor Felix! He went down to the public fountain for water, but all he brought back was a black eye. One fist landed plum in the centre. It is as black as our kitchen. The crowd at the fountain was angry that he took two buckets.

Chius has a bad bruise too where one of the donkeys kicked him. He was trying to get the halter over the donkeys' necks to lead them to the millstone. But they were upset and would not stand still.

Even the sea is restless. Samius went down to the holitorium to complain about the grain. Chius found weevils in it when he tipped it out yesterday. While it was being weighed, Samius heard a sailor say that the waves are as high as Neptune's trident. Yet there is little breeze. How can anyone not think that the gods are angry? If Father says again that tremors are common in Pompeii, I will scream. It is the third day now that the ground has shaken. This is not common, is it? Are I – and an old man – the only people in Pompeii who think that something is amiss?

The papyrus is trembling on my bed – yet there is no breeze at all now. The tremors have begun again. Oh Isis, *when* will it end?

23 October

I must write quickly, before the oil in my lamp runs out, though I can hardly bear what I must write now.

I have seen Aengus. He has escaped from the gladiators' barracks. That at least makes me happy, but it is terrible what he told me. He was to have fought – a fight to entertain the baker Vastus and his guests! I will never speak a word to Vastus again. Never! I thank Isis that Aengus escaped. He would surely have been killed. I pray he is not caught and is now far away from Pompeii. Isis, I pray you speed him safely on his journey.

But I will miss him. Oh how I will miss him. I will never see him again. Never. Oh Claudia, you have smudged the papyrus again. Claudia, stop crying!

I can hear sobs through the wall. Sextus is crying too. Like me he cannot sleep – though save that cat mewling outside it is quiet now. The thunder frightened him – as it frightened us all – a clap of thunder so loud it sounded as if Jupiter had hurled his thunderbolt straight at Pompeii. And the ground shook again – how it shook. It has quite spoiled the plasterer's work.

But I will try not to think about that now. I must tell you how I came to see Aengus again. I was in the stable, comforting the donkeys, when I heard a sound that I never thought to hear again. An owl-hoot. At first I thought I had dreamed it, and then it came again – louder this time. I opened the side gate and looked outside. I looked both left and right, but I could not see anyone. I was about to go back in when I heard it again. I shut the gate and crept down the street. Again, that owl-hoot. I followed it and it led me along until I reached an alley. And there I saw Aengus, crouching behind a heap of builders' rubble.

How I started! "Aengus," I said at last. All sorts of questions tumbled through my mind. How did he escape? Why was he here? Why did he not run?

I opened my mouth to speak, but Aengus put a finger to his lips. I looked nervously up and down the street to see if anyone was watching. But no one was about.

"The charioteer helped me escape," he said hurriedly. "I saved his life in the arena, so he tried to save mine. He heard the lanista say that I was to fight." Aengus stopped and a half smile twisted his face. "It would not be a fair fight. I was to face the best gladiator in Pompeii – to entertain the baker Vastus's guests."

I felt sick. "But – how – why," I got out.

"He said," Aengus stopped and I saw him swallow. "Let us see if that British barbarian fights as well on foot as he drives

131

the chariot. Let us see if he shows as much courage when he faces the Murmillo."

Tears filled my eyes. I blinked them away. Aengus must leave Pompeii, and he could never return. I must tell him so too, I must tell him to leave this very minute and I could not bear to.

"I must leave now," Aengus said, as if he had read my mind. "I am glad I saw you again, Claudia. I am glad you heard my call. I did not want to leave without wishing you farewell."

I nodded. I could not speak.

And then I felt the ground shudder again. We both looked down. "This is a terrible place," Aengus said. "You should leave too, Claudia. Have you not seen how upset the animals are? They are telling us that all is not well."

"I know," I said. "Some say that the giants are stirring again." Or even Vulcan himself, I thought to myself, remembering my dream, remembering what I'd thought that day in the Forum – the day the ground shook over a year ago.

"Giants?" Aengus said, sounding surprised. "No, that," he pointed at Vesuvius. "That is waking up."

Together we turned to look at the great mountain.

Then we turned to look at each other, and I forgot all about the trembling ground. And Vesuvius – and whatever fate Vulcan had in store for us. My face felt hot.

Aengus hesitated. "I wish – I wish you could come with me, Claudia. Would you?" He held out his hand. I reached for it. For a long minute we stood, hands clasped tightly.

But then I remembered little Sextus, and Marcus. And Mother and Father. I could not leave them. My eyes filled again, and my hand dropped back to my side.

"I cannot," I said softly. "I am sorry. I must stay with my family."

Aengus smiled, but it was a sad smile. "You are a good Roman girl, Claudia."

I slipped off the bulla I always wore and handed it to him. "Wear it," I said. "It will protect you."

"I will wear it always," he said. He slipped off the leather thong I'd given him from around his neck and I put it around mine.

Oh, how sadly we looked at each other.

"Leave Pompeii, Claudia," Aengus suddenly said, urgently. "Leave now – while there is still time."

Tears began to run down my cheeks.

"I will always be with you," he said softly. "Wherever you are, wherever you go."

"I will *never* forget you," I said chokingly.

I stood and watched as he ran away from me. I watched until I could see him no more. "May the gods go with you, Aengus," I whispered. Then slowly I made my way back down the alley and in through the side gate.

When Father returned from Vastus's banquet, he told us that a gladiator had escaped. How he escaped no one knows. But he will surely be brought back, Father says. Oh Isis,

I pray you that by now Aengus is far away from Pompeii. Now I must stop writing. My lamp is flickering so feebly that I can barely see the papyrus at all.

24 October

Early morning

I am writing perched near the window to catch the dawn light. It is still quiet. Oddly, not even the birds are singing. At the end of the bed, Fausta is still asleep. Earlier, lying here – half-awake, half-asleep – I swear I heard an owl-hoot. Aengus, I thought joyfully. He has not left. He has come back for me. I tiptoed to the window and opened the shutter. I peered out eagerly. The moon had sunk nearly out of sight, but even so I could see that there was no one there. Hopelessly I stared and stared into the empty street. I felt so sad then – sad and utterly alone.

I crept back to bed, and I must have dozed then for suddenly I felt myself jerk fully awake. The shutters were rattling. The house seemed to groan. I crawled down the bed and huddled next to Fausta. She put an arm over me and at last I slept. But what awful dreams I had then. Awful frightening dreams. I was relieved to wake.

I can hear voices now – angry voices – complaining loudly. A crowd has gathered outside – bakery customers. Why is the bakery not open? they demand. Why is there no water?

Surely they do not blame Father for *that*?

But why is there no water? Why is the bakery not open? Like a hot dry wave, fear sweeps over me.

The earth is trembling again and Mother is calling. I must put away my diary for now.

Afternoon

I am trying to write neatly, but it isn't easy. I have my diary on my knees and my letters are all wobbly. Marcus has been peering at it, and I did not want him to. So I wrote something I *did* want him to see:

MARCUS, STOP READING WHAT IS NOT FOR YOUR EYES

He is most annoyed and has wandered off now to buy figs. Sextus is hiding behind the wagon. He is playing with some other small children whose families have taken shelter here, and I am pretending I cannot see him. Father has gone to find water. How strange it is to write that, as if this was just an ordinary day, yet this has been the most terrible unordinary day of my life, frightening me half out of my mind. Below us, the sea glitters in the sunshine. But to the east, it is as if Vulcan has drawn a dark blanket over the sky, hiding Pompeii and half the bay from us. How odd it was to come out of that into this. Refugees from Pompeii are still crawling into the town. Some can barely walk. Some clasp precious bundles, others, weeping, clutch torches that have long gone out. Their faces and clothes are cloaked grey with ash, their bodies drooping and bowed, like a long funeral procession. But their eyes – I can hardly bear to look at them – filled with the horror of what they have seen. I search their faces for Felix, for Aemilia – for *anyone* we know.

A small crowd of boys has gathered near the wagon to stare at Vesuvius, the black cloud towering over it, ripped now by sheets of flame. Earlier I heard Marcus boast airily about our escape – as if he'd forgotten how frightened he was. Anyway, we haven't escaped – not yet. Hasn't he noticed that evil cloud hovering over our heads like a giant spreading mushroom?

Why is Father taking so long to return? All around me people are looking anxious. They have noticed that big cloud even if Father hasn't. A man leads his weeping wife past. She has one hand clasped over her tummy. A child is growing inside. A small child clings to her other hand. "We will go to the beach," I hear her husband say comfortingly. "We will shelter in the caves. It will be safer there than here." And – oh, Isis! I fear he is right! I can taste ash in my mouth, and on my knees the roll of papyrus is shaking slightly. The ground has begun to tremble again.

But I forget! I have not yet told you why we are here.

I must return to where I stopped this morning – to when we learned that the town's water supply had failed.

That was when we should have left. I can still see Father pacing restlessly up and down. A long time had passed since he'd sent Felix out for water. When at last Felix returned, he was breathless. He tipped the bucket over on its head. Nothing! Crowds had gathered round the public fountains, he panted. Rumours were flying all around the town. Some said that the town's aqueduct would soon be repaired. Others that we had angered the gods, and that it would be many days before we had water again. So, Felix told us, he ran all the way to the Forum to see what he could learn from the town authorities. Oh loyal Felix! There he saw a notice signed by the magistrates announcing that the water supply would be turned back on in a few hours' time.

Father was still looking thoughtful. "The town's water supply failed at the time of the Great Earthquake," he said. "When it is restored is not the principal issue here. It is the *cause* that must concern us." His voice rapped out. "Harness the donkeys to the wagon."

Mother looked bewildered. "But why? Are we leaving Pompeii? Where will we go? Are we not safe here?"

Father shook his head, pointing out the fresh cracks. "Look at them," he said. "I fear the house will not withstand another great earthquake. We must find somewhere safer to shelter, in the countryside, or on the coast. If the gods are willing we will return soon."

"Let us first consult the gods," Mother pleaded. "Let us see what their will is."

"Wife, we have had warnings aplenty," Father said. "We must heed them. We will make a sacrifice before we leave and pray that the gods grant us a safe journey."

Then he saw me staring. "Go, Claudia," he ordered me. "Unchain Pollux."

I ran to do his bidding. I should have been pleased that Father was heeding the warnings, but I felt more scared than anything else. In the bakery Pollux was walking round and round restlessly. He would not stand still. My hands trembled as I wrestled with his chain. I could not undo it.

Someone's big hands gently moved mine aside. I looked up to see Samius. Deftly he untangled the chain. "Useless dog," he growled, but he was smiling as he put the terrified Pollux into my arms.

The wagon was packed and we were ready to leave – precious vessels, bronze and silverware hastily wrapped in cloths and put away, the strongbox securely locked. Father swung himself up into his seat.

Samius hurried in, his face beaming. "The water is flowing again," he said. "Look, Master." He held out a beaker, tipping it slightly so that water dripped on to the floor. So Felix was sent back to the fountain for water. I perched restlessly on the wagon. Why, oh why, this fresh delay? Could we not collect water on our way?

The ground began to tremble again. "Enough," growled Father at last. "We must delay no longer."

But could we get the donkeys to move? No! In vain Father pulled on the reins. In vain he urged them on. It was I who suggested blindfolding them.

The wagon jolted forwards. Father smiled proudly at me. "My clever little Claudia," he said.

Father had asked Samius and the bakery slaves if they wished to leave too. Mother looked at Father as if he had gone mad, but Samius stood firm. In vain Father protested that he should take his family away. "We will be safe enough here," he said, stubbornly. "The tremors will pass. And someone has to bake the bread. I cannot leave it to that dolt Chius." Father looked at Samius, as if he had never seen him properly before. And Chius says he will guard the bakery for us. Dear Chius! Father says he will see about his freedom when we return.

When we return, Father had said. I drew comfort from those words as our wagon trundled down the street.

An odd sight we must have seemed to those people going about their daily business as usual. Eight of us – our whole family and our household slaves – squashed in amongst chests, cushions and blankets.

Our route took us past Vastus's new bakery. The man serving at the counter stared at us – surprise written all over his face. Mother dared not complain but the bitterness on her face showed well what she thought. *Their* business has opened as usual. *They* will not run away merely because the water supply failed for a few hours. That is why Vastus is a richer man than you.

We were barely past the bakery when a blast of hot air whistled past us, the dust cloud in its wake making us gasp like fishes. From the north came an enormous crash – as if something far away had exploded. "What was that?" Mother gasped. The donkeys bucked and brayed. Father pulled hard on the reins, shouting back to us to hold on tight.

All around us people had stopped what they were doing, standing as still as if turned to stone. Here a man, hammer raised in an outstretched arm. There, a woman, her basket upturned, its contents spilled out on to the ground. All eyes were on the far-off mountain. Grey-white streaks drifted down one side – like drifts of snow or flecks of ash. I stared. I had not noticed that before. But it was not that that held my eyes. What was it – that *thing* – that brown column shooting out of the top of Vesuvius, like a pillar or a vast tree trunk? Higher and higher it climbed, while I craned my neck back further and further to see it. Stupidly I thought that Vulcan had punched a hole in the mountain top. A giant rumble – was Vulcan laughing at us? – rolled down the mountain.

Next to me on the wagon the boys screamed. But I did not utter a sound. The mountain still had me in its spell. I could not take my eyes off that thing blazing out of the top of Vesuvius.

Like branches on an enormous pine tree, cloud billowed out from the great smoky column, which was still climbing, higher, ever higher into the sky. Cloud streaked brown in patches.

I heard myself gasp. "The mountain is exploding."

"Aye, child," a voice next to me said. "Vesuvius has woken." Ancient! What was he doing here? The old man sniffed the air. "The wind has changed. It is coming from the north-west. Go west, child, as far and fast as you can. Out of the path of that." He raised his stick and pointed it at the cloud.

I remembered what Ancient had said the last time I'd seen him. "The gods will tell me when and where to go."

What did he mean? What danger did that roiling cloud hold for us?

I stared at the mountain. The column was still climbing, but the cloud was rolling down across the mountain now – towards us! And it was as if the spell had been broken. People who had stood silently watching began to run, shoving past the wagon, elbowing each other aside in their haste to escape the thing now thundering across the plain – a huge rumbling billowing cloud.

Father hit the donkeys, but they needed little encouragement. If it had not been for the crush of people I am sure they'd have bolted. I leaned over the side of the wagon and grabbed Ancient's hand as the wagon jerked forward.

"Come with us," I cried.

Ancient smiled, looking at the heaped wagon. "We will make room for you. I can walk," I said stoutly.

"Nay, child, I will not take your place in your father's wagon," he said. "All my life I have gone at my own pace, and I will do so now."

"Oh, Ancient," I cried sadly, feeling his hand slip out of mine. And then he was gone. Had he fallen, knocked to the ground by the people stampeding past? Or was that him I saw, hobbling down a side street, away from the terrified people surging south, down the hill towards the Stabian Gate.

I crouched down in the wagon, grateful for its shelter.

"Think you'll escape the gods' wrath in that wagon, eh?" a man mocked. He held a silver vessel in his arms – stolen I felt sure. I gave him a haughty look, but he merely laughed as he vanished into the crowd ahead of us. Sextus began to sob. I pulled him close and stroked his head, trying to comfort him, trying to stifle my own fear. That man had been right. We'd do better on foot.

Father pulled hard on the reins, bringing the wagon to a halt. I saw him turn in his seat to stare at the cloud still racing towards us. "The wind blows from the north-west," he said as Ancient had. "Very well then." He scanned the darkening sky. "It is a gamble but… We must turn round, and head west, out of its path."

The donkeys stumbled forward again. Rocking slightly the wagon began to roll down the hill. Like a ship caught on the edge of a whirlpool we were slowly being pulled south. I heard the donkeys bray as Father tugged the reins, trying to turn their heads. The wagon rocked up and down. Father cursed. "I cannot turn the wagon," he shouted back to us. "I will get down and try to lead the donkeys round."

I watched as Father jumped down, the reins still in his hands. For one awful moment, his head vanished from sight and I feared he'd been swept away in the crowd. Oh the relief to see his face again.

The wagon rocked back and forth. Father wiped his sweating face. "It is too heavy to turn," he called. "All of you, save Sextus and Fausta, get down and help me push it round."

I handed the whimpering Pollux to Sextus and clambered down, sheltering as best I could against the wagon, my back bumping painfully against it as people pushed past, swearing and cursing. Such looks they gave us! The wagon had almost completely blocked the road. "On the third count push – push as hard as you can," Father shouted. "One. Two. Three," he bawled. I leaned my shoulder hard against the wagon and heaved. The wagon creaked and rocked on its axles, up and down, up and down, but at last, slowly, it turned. Then we had to help push it up the hill again. By the time we had reached the top my shoulder was aching and my tunic sticking to me front and back.

Father helped us clamber up again. "Up you go," he said, as cheerily as if we were on an outing to the country rather than fleeing for our lives. We joined a long line of people shuffling along the road north-west towards the Herculaneum Gate.

I peered around. The sky was still thundering overhead. People darted in and out of doorways, clutching children, alarm clear on their faces. Over to our left now was the road that led to the Marine Gate and the port – as choked with fleeing people as the road south. Most took that route, those that could not fight their way south. Were we mad, those of us fleeing north, right into the path of the storm?

As we passed the street where we would usually turn for home Mother cried out: "Where are you taking us? Are we not going home?"

"We are going to Herculaneum," Father said firmly.

"If we must go on, should we not try to escape by ship?" Mother pleaded.

"We will never escape that way," Father said. "The fleet is stationed at the north of the bay. Even supposing word of this disaster has yet reached the admiral, how long do you think it will be before the fleet reaches us? Even supposing it can. Or should we hire a fishing boat?"

Mother was silent.

Past the Forum now, its colonnades rising like stumps over the buildings to my left. Left now, or was it right? Down a wide road, now crawling along an alley so narrow I feared we'd stick fast. North, veering west. I looked up fearfully. How dark the sky was growing – darker and darker the closer that cloud drew to us. I call it a cloud for I cannot think of a better word for it. But clouds do not make a noise, and this sounded as if countless warhorses were galloping inside it. And we – we were driving right into the heart of that storm! I heard Marcus scream – his words barely audible above the din. "The cloud! It is nearly upon us." I gripped the sides of the wagon tightly. Hurry, I prayed. Oh, hurry! Ash began to fall, spattering us like dry snow. And then – plop – something landed next to me in the wagon. Then plop again – on my cheek. It stung. I put up my hand and touched my face. My fingers came away wet. Blood! Another stone dropped down next to me. I picked it up and felt it, weighing it in my hand. It was greyish white, small and light, and as filled with holes as a sea sponge. Pumice! The sky was raining ash and pumice!

"What are you doing? Lie down, foolish child," I heard Mother cry. She threw a blanket towards me and I pulled it over my head. Next to me, Sextus was whimpering. Pollux huddled in the crook of my drawn-up legs, his body juddering against them. Mother was murmuring. "We should never have left home. We'd have been safer there. Oh, Isis. Isis, help us!" Under the blanket I felt the pumice falling – pummelling my head and back, arms and legs. Tears began to trickle down my cheeks. Angrily I rubbed them away, but they would not stop falling. Tears for us, and for everyone fleeing my beloved Pompeii.

The blanket was getting heavy. I lifted it up to shake off the pumice, feeling it roll down and bounce off the wagon.

I lay back down, shaking. Such sights I'd seen in the brief moment I'd held the blanket up. Frothy pumice and ash spattering the roads, pounding roofs and buildings. People sheltering in doorways, hammering on doors, begging for help. Before I lay back down again I saw one open a crack. A hand emerged to pull a person hurriedly inside. Gusts of ash swirled in the entrance before the door slammed shut. It was now almost completely dark.

Ahead now, a fountain. We stopped and I saw Father run across to it for water, a blanket flapping round his head and shoulders. Someone lit a torch and as it flared into life I saw an old woman bent over, leaning in close to the fountainhead to drink. When she straightened up again, I realized that she was not old at all. It was ash that had turned her hair grey. There was no sign of Felix. I ducked down under my blanket. I felt as if the city was under siege, as if a huge army had ranged outside the gates and was catapulting pumice at us from giant ballistas and slingshots. Had the gods abandoned us? Was the whole world about to end?

At the Herculaneum Gate we had to stop again. What now? I wondered despairingly. Would we ever reach safety? I pulled back the blanket again. Just inside the gate, a wagon had stuck fast.

Father shouted at the driver to move aside but he waved his arms helplessly. He pointed to his mules and shrugged. They would not move. In the torchlight I saw the mules'

146

heads rear, their eyes maddened with fear. Why did the driver not cover their eyes? The poor creatures were terrified. I watched as Father tore strips off his cloak and thrust them into the driver's hands.

"In the name of Jupiter, bandage their eyes," he shouted. "If you wish ever to move again." I watched as the driver grabbed first one mule's head, then the other, wrapping their eyes tightly with the cloth.

The driver clambered back into his seat. Would his wagon move now? Would it? What if it didn't? I felt myself shudder, imagining our fate. We'd have to abandon our wagon, clamber down, be hurled into that sea of people. We'd surely lose each other. Be sorely battered too by the falling rock and ash. And then I felt the wagon lurch. We were moving! We were through the gate. Relief made me cry again.

"Thank you, thank you, Isis," I sobbed.

We were travelling through the great cemetery that lay outside the gate, but for once I was not afraid of the dead. The living frightened me more. On all sides I could hear wails and shouts. Fingers clawed the wagon, tipping off the pumice, wrenching at the blankets. We clung to them, in our fear cruelly pushing the hands away. "Help us! Help us!" Muffled voices. Father shouted something down to us, and I pushed up the blanket a little so that I could hear him, feeling the stones rattle off my blanket on to the ground.

"I cannot get the donkeys to move," he bawled.

I pulled up a corner of the blanket fully – and gasped. The sky was still thundering over our heads but now it was utterly black. I waved my hand in front of my face, but I could not see it at all. A dense dark cloud was spreading over the earth like a flood. How can I describe it? It was darker than a cloudy night, as dark as a closed room, in which all the lamps had been put out.

Mother was shouting at me to lie down, but I pretended I couldn't hear her. My heart was thumping but I knew what I had to do. We could not stay here like this. We'd die under the weight of stones and rocks showering down on us. I pushed Pollux away, wrapped a blanket round me and edged myself over the side of the wagon. As I jumped I wondered how far I would fall. I have always hated the dark, and I could still see nothing at all. My foot jarred as it hit the ground. In my ears still that steady rumbling. Pumice pounded my blanketed head and shoulders as I edged slowly forward – feeling under my fingers the wood of the wagon become the rough coat of a donkey. Somehow I hoisted myself up again, sliding forwards on to the donkey's back. I could not even see that, and when I looked back, the wagon seemed to have vanished. Choking down my terror, I felt my way along the donkey's back until I could lay my head close against its neck. I pulled the blanket over us both, feeling the donkey's rough and dusty mane against my cheek. But now that I was there I did not know what to say. I murmured to the donkey softly, but it did not move. It did not listen. Tears began

148

to slide down my cheeks. I stroked the donkey's mane. If only Aengus were here. If only… He would know what to say. He would know how to get the donkeys moving again.

It felt like hours that I lay there, helplessly clasping the donkey's neck. And then I began to have the strangest sense that I was not alone any more. That Aengus was guiding me. What had he said to me? "A good horseman is guided by his horse." I do not know what I said or did then, but as if by a miracle the donkeys started forwards again. I sobbed with relief, as I lay under the blanket, my arms still clasped tightly round the donkey's neck.

I clambered back on to the wagon, eyes stinging, coughing in the swirling ash. Huddled under my blanket again, I did not feel as if I was on the wagon, my family next to me. I was in that alley near the bakery, listening to what Aengus had said to me that last time. I will always be with you, he had told me. Wherever you are. Wherever you go. Do not be afraid, his voice seemed to be whispering in my ear. I am with you.

How long we lay there, bouncing painfully in the wagon I do not know. Again and again we had to pour pumice off our blankets. Sextus was sick all over himself. More than once I felt the wagon tip and veer sharply off the road and I heard Father swear as he tried to right it again. On our right I knew was the great bulk of Vesuvius. We had not passed out of its shadow yet. On my left the sea sounded as if it was boiling. I thanked the gods – if gods there still be – that we had not attempted to escape that way.

"Look!" Father shouted suddenly. "Look to the west." His voice sounded thick, as if his mouth was full of ash. I stared blankly into the blackness. Where *was* west? What could Father see that I could not? Still shrouded in blankets the boys' heads popped up next to mine. "Look!" they shouted. "Look at the light!" I turned my head until I could see what they did – a faint glimmer of light like a distant dawn or sunset.

"There," Father said and I felt I could hear a smile in his voice. "That is where we will head. Towards that light." We cried and laughed, hugging each other, joyfully. We would escape. We would!

After a time the pumice seemed to be falling less thickly. Cautiously I lifted up a corner of the blanket – and gasped again. Where were we? The blackness had thinned but I felt as if we had been picked up and hurled to some strange far-off country. The land of grey. Everything here was ash grey – grey plants and grey vines poked out from drifts of ash. Next to us, grey-skinned people were stumbling, pushing through a grey desert, staggering under chests and bundles. A wagon had been abandoned, its wheels half sunk into ash and pumice. A dog ran round and round it barking. Somewhere far off I heard a child's teary cry.

I blinked. The column over the mountain seemed to have grown even taller, and the edge of the cloud had billowed west – almost to Herculaneum, the town where we were bound. Had the wind shifted? Was it blowing the pumice-filled cloud further west across the bay? I saw the furrow between Father's eyes deepen as if the same thought was in his mind. And then sunshine burst over my head. The boys shouted and whooped. But it vanished, and again I had to dive under my blanket as pumice spattered the wagon. I felt as if Vulcan was playing a game with us – pretending to let us escape, then casting his black shadow over us again, drawing us back – like the Retiarius netting his prey in the arena.

But not long afterwards I sat up again, squinting like a mole crawling out of its burrow. Ahead of us red-tiled roofs glowed in the sun. Herculaneum. Behind us stretched that grey desert. And beyond it, blackness. Nothing but blackness. I stared and stared, but Pompeii seemed to have vanished.

Someone is shouting and waving at me. It is Father. We are leaving. Father's face looks drawn and anxious. Next to him stands a man I do not know. A bolster is strapped to his head. Red-rimmed eyes peer out of a face as ashy-white as an actor's mask. He sees me staring and calls my name. It is Felix! What good fortune to find him here!

25 October

Very early morning

I thank the gods Mother thought to pack an oil lamp. It is not very comfortable here, but at least we can see. I have crept into a corner of the room to write. Pollux's head is in my lap. My body aches all over. I have a bruise as big as an apple on my arm, and a cut on my face where a stone hit it when I clambered off the wagon.

I do not know what time it is, or even if it is day or night. Father thinks it is morning, but it is still so dark. And I am so tired, I can barely keep my eyes open, but I will keep writing as long as I can. What can be more important than what I write now? I am glad I did not drop my diary. When we had to abandon the wagon I stuffed the scrolls down the front of my tunic.

Marcus's head is cradled on Mother's lap. It is bleeding badly, poor Marcus, but he bears the pain like a true Roman. My mouth is so dry, and I can still taste ash on my tongue. But Father says we must go easy on the water.

Dear Father! If it were not for him, a far worse fate would have befallen us. Of that I am sure.

The ground is not trembling now, and all I can hear is a faint plop plop as pumice strikes the roof and walls. I caught a piece – it is bigger and darker than the stuff that hurtled down on us in Pompeii. Father thinks it comes from deeper inside Vesuvius.

Now I must go back to where I stopped earlier – when we left Herculaneum. Not long after we left the town, the ground shook so violently that we were nearly thrown off the wagon. Behind us lightning flashed out of the black cloud hovering high over Vesuvius. Lightning that forked angrily – like the scarlet tongues of monstrous serpents. On our seaward side we could hear waves crash violently against the shore before being sucked back out to sea again.

Felix helped Father guide the donkeys, but the ground was heaving so badly now that the wagon wobbled first to one side and then the other. "We will have to leave it," Father said wearily at last. He helped me clamber up on to one of the donkeys' backs in front of Fausta. Sextus and Mother rode the other.

Felix talked and talked. Such awful things he told us. Things I will never forget. Words not meant for my ears, but which I heard nevertheless. About people lying injured, calling for help. Others digging themselves out of their homes.

"The roofs were beginning to collapse under the weight of the pumice," Felix said. "I saw children who had lost their parents, fires breaking out, looting..." He swallowed and I tried to shut out the awful picture his words conjured up.

We'd not have escaped by sea, he told us. "I am told that the fleet put out but the ships could not reach the shore for all the pumice floating in the sea. The shore is covered with the stuff too. Rocks, blackened and charred as if burnt. And the waves…" He stretched up his arm. "Higher than a man standing on another man's head."

"And Samius and Chius," Father asked quietly. "Did they take shelter?"

"Aye, that they did," Felix said, "but…" His voice faltered again. Our roof had collapsed and the bakery's too, I felt certain.

"Oh that they had left when we did," I heard Father mutter, his face distressed. I thought about my friends in Pompeii. How many of them had left in time to escape? And what about Uncle, on his farm? "I will live and die on this farm," he had told us. Tears filled my eyes, but I rubbed them away. Uncle did not want my tears. I stared up at the mountain furiously. Hateful Vesuvius! Then I blinked, bewildered. Here and there on the mountain, flames were leaping up, as if torches or fires were being lit. Surely not.

Then, as my eye travelled across the mountain, I saw something else. Something so frightening that I can still see it, in my mind's eye.

Vesuvius seemed to be shrinking. And out of that vast black column of whirling rock and ash a roiling mass of flame emerged like a huge glowing furnace. I shut my eyes, terrified. What was it I had seen? Vulcan's forge itself? All around me I could hear screams. I opened my eyes again. A fiery cloud was hurtling down the side of the mountain. Faster and faster it sped. How loud it sounded – even to us, some miles away.

High over Vesuvius, flames rent the sky, like huge flashes of lightning, as they had in my dream, so long ago. But this was no dream. I could smell burning in my nostrils. Mother was crying that the gods had forsaken us.

"It is heading for Herculaneum," Father shouted hoarsely. I hid my face in my hands. I could not bear to look any more. When I dared to look back again, I could see nothing but blackness where Herculaneum had been. I cried out. The town seemed to have vanished – snuffed out like the wick on my lamp.

It is a wonder that we found this place. No one has knocked on the door asking for shelter. Where are all the people that travelled along the road with us?

I have had the most terrible thought, it is so terrible that I can scarcely bear to write it. It is this: that there is just us left – just us – in the whole of the world. That everything and everyone else has been swallowed up, smothered in the monstrous fiery cloud that we saw sweep down Vesuvius. I wish I could push this awful thought away, but I cannot.

Dawn

The wick is flickering on my lamp. I pray it does not go out, not yet. It is still dark, though by now it must surely be dawn.

Father has come over to see what I am doing. I did not turn away. I did not try to hide what I was writing. "Write only what others may read," he told me once.

"See, Father, I have kept a diary." I unrolled the scroll of papyrus to show him. He peered at it.

"What are you writing, child?"

"About what has happened," I told him. "About Pompeii."

"Write, Claudia. Write it all. When the sun rises, we will read it together." He put his hand on my shoulder. I lean back against him and look around the room. Fausta is comforting Xenia and Fortunata. Mother is staring at me, Sextus fast asleep against her shoulder.

When the sun rises… Mother smiles at me and suddenly I remember something she told me, early one morning outside the Temple of Isis. "No matter how dark the night, the sun always rises." I will not forget those words. Not ever. The ground is beginning to shake again, and the wick on my lamp is sputtering but I am not afraid any more. I will hold those words close to me. And now I will put down my pen, roll up the papyrus, and say them aloud, so that everyone will hear them and take comfort. "No matter how dark the night, the sun always rises."

Historical note

When Vesuvius erupted in AD 79 the people living in the cities and towns around the Bay of Naples appear to have been taken completely by surprise. In one house in Pompeii excavators found remains of a hastily abandoned meal. In a bakery 81 overcooked loaves were discovered in an oven. No one knew that they were living in the shadow of an active volcano, and that it was about to erupt. Early in AD 62 there had been a major earthquake that destroyed much of Pompeii and the nearby city of Herculaneum. But no one in those days understood the connection between earthquakes and volcanic eruption.

Even educated Romans like Pliny the Younger, who was seventeen at the time of the eruption, merely noted that earthquakes were common in the region. His uncle, Pliny the Elder, admiral of the Roman fleet, had written a 37-volume "Natural History", but he too was unaware of the link between earthquakes and volcanic eruption.

There had been more recent warnings that Vesuvius was about to erupt. In the four days preceding the eruption Pompeii had been shaken by earth tremors. Wells and springs had dried up. On the morning of the eruption itself the city's water supply failed due to earthquake damage. This had happened at the time of the big earthquake in AD 62. Fumaroles (plumes of gas) were seen. The more superstitious inhabitants interpreted these as signs that the giants were stirring. The giants were supposed to have been buried under the mountain by the gods. Their stirrings were believed to herald a volcanic eruption – a terrifying prospect. But on the whole, at the time of the eruption people were carrying on with their lives as they always had. Builders and plasterers were found to repair cracks caused by the fresh earth tremors, and damaged wall frescoes were repainted.

Early one morning, four days after the tremors began, there was a minor blast from the volcano. Then, at around one o'clock, Vesuvius erupted. The eruption was visible as far away as Misenum, at the north end of the Bay of Naples where the Roman fleet was stationed. A giant cloud, filled with hot ash and pumice, burst out of the top of Vesuvius.

At his uncle's house at Misenum, Pliny the Younger saw it all. It looked like "a pine tree, for it shot up to a great height in the form of a trunk, which extended itself at the top into several branches" he later wrote to his friend, the Roman historian Tacitus. Pliny wrote two letters to Tacitus about the eruption. They are our only eyewitness accounts and tell us a great deal about it and how people felt and acted at the time.

Nowadays "seismic" (earthquake) activity is carefully

monitored by volcanologists. They are able to tell weeks or even months in advance when a volcanic eruption is likely to take place, so that people can be safely evacuated. But the inhabitants of Pompeii had no such warning, and no plans for their evacuation could be made.

They must have been both terrified and bewildered as they looked up at Vesuvius. Ash and pumice was being ejected from the volcano at a terrifying rate – around 1,000 kph. The wind was blowing from the north-west – bringing the full force of the eruption right over Pompeii. The column of ash and pumice over Vesuvius would rise gradually higher and higher during that day, until it reached a peak of around 33 km. Ash and pumice bombarded Pompeii, making escape difficult for the inhabitants, and eventually causing roofs and buildings to collapse. During the afternoon the cloud of hot ash and pumice plunged the city into darkness. Many believed that the gods had deserted them, or even that the world was ending.

The nearby city of Herculaneum escaped most of the fallout of ash and pumice but was shaken by the earth tremors that shook Pompeii. As these worsened, people fled – many making their way down to the beach to seek shelter there, perhaps even hoping for rescue by sea. But it was impossible for anyone to escape by sea. The volcanic matter that bombarded Pompeii had landed in the sea, too, until it was so densely filled by floating pumice that the fleet

– that set out to rescue the inhabitants – had to abandon the attempt. Admiral Pliny, who accompanied the fleet, ordered it to sail on to Stabiae. Fascinated by the eruption he remained at Stabiae, finally perishing there on the beach.

At night the pattern of the eruption changed. Volcanic matter was being ejected from Vesuvius at an enormous rate – around 150,000 tonnes per second – and from much deeper inside the volcano. The density of the column over Vesuvius was such that it now began to collapse. Meanwhile, the earth tremors were becoming more violent. Tidal waves lashed the coast. There were lightning flashes, caused by friction of the volcanic particles.

Early the next morning, the first of several "pyroclastic" flows and surges occurred. A vast burning cloud raced down Vesuvius towards Herculaneum. In a matter of minutes the cloud of hot ash, volcanic rock and gas had overrun the city. The ferocious heat – 500°C or more – would have killed anyone still in the city or sheltering on the beach instantly. It was followed a few minutes later by a second pyroclastic surge. This also killed the inhabitants of the nearby towns of Terzigno and Oplontis. Herculaneum was now completely buried under 25 metres of volcanic debris, which was to harden over time into solid rock, making later excavation very difficult.

Around dawn the roasting, gas-filled volcanic surge reached the walls of Pompeii. The next pyroclastic surge overran the walls, killing everyone still sheltering in the city. A fifth surge overran Pompeii again, burying the city completely. The final surge – a short while afterwards – was the biggest of all. The volcano had finally collapsed and the surge spread over a much wider area, killing many of those who had fled the city earlier. The impact of this surge was felt as far away as Misenum, where darkness fell and buildings shook so badly that the inhabitants – including Pliny the Younger and his mother – were forced to flee their homes.

Later that morning mud rain began to fall. The air began to clear. At Misenum Pliny noted that the sun was "yellowish, as it is during an eclipse". It shone on a grey desert; a wasteland of ash and pumice. The shore had receded. The city of Pompeii had disappeared – buried under around 3–5 metres of volcanic debris, with perhaps the tips of the tallest buildings like the amphitheatre just visible to show where the city had been. Herculaneum, Oplontis and Terzigno, and the luxurious villas that had dotted the coast, had utterly vanished.

When news of the disaster reached Rome, Emperor Titus ordered search parties to the area to dig for survivors. But after a few days the search was abandoned. Plans to rebuild the cities were shelved. The cities were too deeply submerged under rock and ash. Looters helped themselves to what treasure they could find.

It is still not known how many perished in the worst-known eruption in Vesuvius's history. The whole region was affected. Even now bodies are being discovered.

For hundreds of years the vanished cities of Pompeii and Herculaneum lay undisturbed. Italians named the place where Pompeii was thought to be "Civita" (the City).

And then in 1592, while digging a tunnel in the area, an architect called Domenico Fontana discovered the ruins of ancient buildings. He did not know it, but he had stumbled upon Pompeii. In 1689 a stone bearing the inscription "POMPEIA" was found, but the connection with the ancient city of Pompeii was still not made.

It was not until the 18th century that proper excavations began. Spanish engineer Don Rocco de Alcubierre was put in charge of the work. Digging began at Herculaneum in 1739 and nine years later at Pompeii. Excavating was especially difficult at Herculaneum. Tunnels had to be hacked through hard volcanic rock to reach the city. But it was at Herculaneum that De Alcubierre made some major discoveries, including the Forum, the theatre and temples. Unfortunately, though, the excavators were much more interested in the precious objects they found, and a lot of damage was done to the buildings. Frescoes were ripped off walls, statues and other precious objects carted away to furnish the king's palace. The architect Karl Weber, who worked alongside De Alcubierre, fortunately took a more methodical approach to the work, making careful drawings and plans of the buildings he uncovered.

And then in 1763 an inscription was found, finally

proving that the excavators had discovered the lost city of Pompeii. The Temple of Isis was discovered in 1765 and the gladiator barracks shortly afterwards.

In 1772 18 bodies were discovered in an underground room. The discovery caused huge excitement. Scholars visited the cities and wrote enthusiastically about them, though some deplored the unsystematic way the excavations were being undertaken – like a sort of treasure hunt. Wealthy travellers, visiting Italy as part of the "Grand Tour", flocked to the sites of Pompeii and Herculaneum. In 1790 finds from Pompeii and Herculaneum were put in a new national museum in Naples and later displayed to the public. A guidebook to the ruins was published.

In 1860, the king of the newly unified Italy put the archaeologist Giuseppe Fiorelli in charge of excavations at Pompeii. (Archaeologists study the past by examining human and material remains.) Fiorelli's appointment marked the beginning of scientific excavation at Pompeii. He worked out a system that is still used by archaeologists today. The city was divided into regions. Within each region each block and building was given a number. Detailed records of the excavations were kept, and Fiorelli tried to stop finds being removed from the excavations to the Naples museum.

And Fiorelli made a very important discovery – cavities in the hardened ash. By filling them with plaster he discovered that the cavities were what had been left behind after organic matter had decayed. The shapes of people, animals, plants, trees, even a person's clothing and missing parts of furniture could be revealed by this method.

Later archaeologists carried on Fiorelli's work, trying to protect houses and their contents by carefully restoring the buildings. The work of conserving already excavated buildings began. One of the most famous archaeologists associated with Pompeii is Amedeo Maiuri. He made many important discoveries. By digging down deeper, he found evidence that the city had been occupied long before Roman times.

Not just grand buildings, important temples and statues have been discovered at Pompeii and Herculaneum. Over 30 bakeries, as well as many workshops, laundries and ordinary homes have been identified. The intense heat from the pyroclastic surges helped preserve all sorts of things that would usually decay over time. Little things, like wooden bed-frames, loaves of bread, fish bones in the fish market, a meal hastily abandoned – that add so much to our understanding of the Roman way of life. In a house next to a bakery – which archaeologists have named "the House of the Chaste Lovers" after the frescoes painted in one of the rooms – paint pots still full of dried paint were found, dropped when the painters fled the eruption.

The sites are in a fragile state. Bombs dropped in the area during the Second World War, more recent earthquakes and eruptions have added to the damage done to the cities by the early excavators and made the job of archaeologists more difficult. Long exposure to the elements and tourism has also had a bad effect on the excavated areas, leading to further deterioration of already fragile buildings. Modern archaeological techniques are better able to handle the work of restoring and conserving the remains – but they are costly.

Much of the towns still lie buried, under modern buildings, and we will never see the whole of them. But what has been discovered has added enormously to our knowledge and understanding of the Romans, and opened a window on to a fascinating world that came to an abrupt end that day in AD 79.

Recent research

Very recent research has proved conclusively that the traditional date given for the eruption of Vesuvius in AD 79 – 24 August – is incorrect. The eruption occurred later in the year, probably on 24 October. This is the date used in Claudia's diary.

A note on Roman time

The Roman day was divided up into two periods of 12 hours. The first began at sunrise, and ended at sunset, the second began at sunset, ending at sunrise the following day. This meant that the length of a Roman hour varied depending on the season.

Timeline

BC

circa 8th century Evidence of Iron Age settlement at Pompeii.

circa 550 The town of Pompeii is founded, possibly by a tribe known as the Oscans. The settlement is built on a lava flow from a much earlier eruption.

474 The Greeks rule the Bay of Naples. Pompeii is a flourishing town. Temples are built and the town is fortified.

420s The Samnites, a southern Italian mountain tribe, conquer the area. The people of the area become known as Campanians. Pompeii is refortified, with towers added to the town walls.

290 The Roman Republic conquers central Italy.

90 Campanian towns, including Pompeii, rebel against Roman rule, but are defeated by the Romans under their general, Sulla.

89 Sulla occupies the town of Pompeii. Its townspeople, like other peoples conquered by the Romans, are granted Roman citizenship.

80 Pompeii becomes a Roman colony.

AD

62 An earthquake destroys much of Herculaneum and Pompeii.

79 Vesuvius erupts, burying Pompeii, Herculaneum and much of the region around the Bay of Naples.

104 Pliny the Younger writes two letters to his friend, the historian Tacitus, in which he describes the eruption.

1592 Domenico Fontana, a Roman architect, finds ruins while digging a canal. He has found the ancient city of Pompeii, but the significance of his discovery is not understood.

1689 A stone is found, bearing the inscription "Pompeia".

1739 Spanish engineer Don Rocco de Alcubierre excavates the sites of what are later identified as the buried cities of Herculaneum and Pompeii. Architects like Karl Weber take a more systematic approach to the excavations, recording their finds in detail.

1763 The inscription "Pompeii" is found on a tomb, finally identifying the city as Pompeii.

1860 Following the unification of Italy into one kingdom, scientific excavations begin at Pompeii under the archaeologist Giuseppe Fiorelli.

1924–1961 Amedeo Maiuri is put in charge of the excavations. He finds the remains of earlier settlements at Pompeii.

1980 An earthquake further damages the sites. Emphasis is placed on recording, restoration and conservation of the sites.

Portrait of a 1st century AD Pompeiian couple, possibly Terentius Neo and his wife. He may have been a baker.

Bread being sold to customers. Over 30 bakeries have been excavated in Pompeii. Some bakers handled all milling and baking processes on site – from grinding the grain to baking the bread. Bread could also be sold separately, in a shop or direct to the customer.

Ruins of the Forum at Pompeii. The Forum was the centre of a Roman town. Here were the most important public buildings, and temples, and where the town was governed and laws administered. It was also a place to meet and a flourishing market.

Built some time after 70 BC, the stone amphitheatre at Pompeii is the oldest-known in the Roman world. In it around 20,000 spectators could watch the games, gladiator and wild beast fights and criminals being executed.

Pompeii didn't have a modern drainage system. Everything flowed down the streets. Raised pavements and crossing stones meant that pedestrians didn't have to walk through the rubbish. The ruts you can see were caused by iron bands on cart wheels wearing away the stone.

Vesuvius has erupted many times since the famous eruption of
AD 79. This painting shows an eruption in the 1770s.

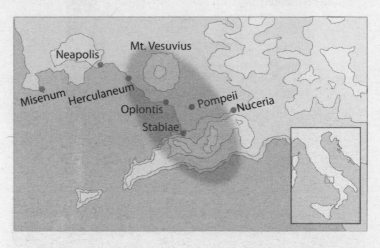

This map shows the initial fallout from Vesuvius's eruption in
AD 79. Later, pyroclastic flows and surges devastated a much
wider area. Pliny the Younger even felt the impact of the eruption
at Misenum. Ash fell as far away as Africa.

The archaeologist Fiorelli discovered that by filling cavities left in the hardened ash with plaster he could reveal the shapes of the bodies of people who perished in the eruption in Pompeii in AD 79.

Spectators watch the Temple of Isis being excavated. In the 18th century wealthy travellers on the Grand Tour flocked to Pompeii and Herculaneum.

Acknowledgement

I would like to thank Paul Roberts, of the British Museum's department of Greek and Roman Antiquities, for his help with my research for this book.

Picture acknowledgments

P 168 The Art Archive/Musée Archéologique Naples/Alfredo Dagli Orti
P 168 The Art Archive/Musée Archéologique Naples/Alfredo Dagli Ortii
P 168 CORBIS/Roger Ressmeyer
P 169 CORBIS/Gian Berto Vanni
P 169 Werner Forman Archive/Location
P 170 (top) Heritage-Images/Ann Ronan
P 171 CORBIS/Bettmann
P 171 Heritage-Images/British Library

Experience history first-hand with My Story –
a series of vividly imagined accounts of life in the past.

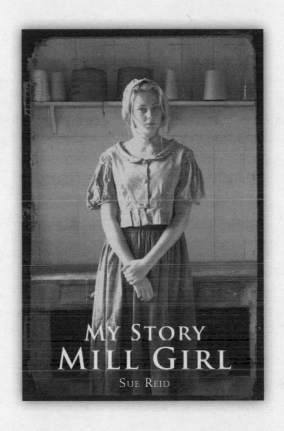

My Story
MILL GIRL
SUE REID

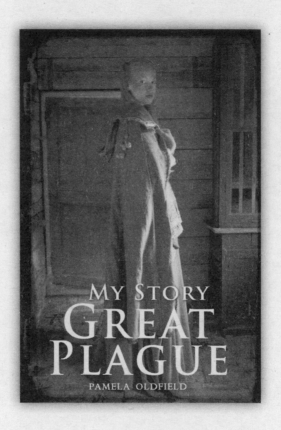

MY STORY
GREAT
PLAGUE

PAMELA OLDFIELD